D1783819

# IMPULSE

*Also available from Headline Liaison*

Possession by Kay Cavendish
Stolen Passions by Kay Cavendish
The Journal by James Allen
Love Letters by James Allen
The Diary by James Allen
Out of Control by Rebecca Ambrose
Aphrodisia by Rebecca Ambrose
A Private Affair by Carol Anderson
Voluptuous Voyage by Lacey Carlyle
Magnolia Moon by Lacey Carlyle
Vermilion Gates by Lucinda Chester
The Challenge by Lucinda Chester
Spring Fever by Lucinda Chester
The Paradise Garden by Aurelia Clifford
Hearts on Fire by Tom Crewe and Amber Wells
Sleepless Nights by Tom Crewe and Amber Wells
Dangerous Desires by J J Duke
Seven Days by J J Duke
A Scent of Danger by Sarah Hope-Walker
Private Lessons by Cheryl Mildenhall
Intimate Strangers by Cheryl Mildenhall
Dance of Desire by Cheryl Mildenhall

# Impulse

Kay Cavendish

HEADLINE
Liaison

First published in 1997
by HEADLINE BOOK PUBLISHING

A HEADLINE LIAISON paperback

10 9 8 7 6 5 4 3 2 1

ISBN 0 7472 5473 7

Typeset by CBS, Felixstowe, Suffolk

Printed and bound in Great Britain by
Cox & Wyman Ltd, Reading, Berks

HEADLINE BOOK PUBLISHING
A division of Hodder Headline PLC
338 Euston Road
London NW1 3BH

# Impulse

# *One*

Ariane met him when she was practising the part of 'company wife' for Jon. They were at a reception-come-garden party held at a stately home. A combination of *Brideshead Revisited* and Ascot on Ladies' day, the setting had been chosen specifically to impress the firm's new American partners. Jon, Ariane's fiancé, was the Finance Director and much of his time was spent on company business.

Intent on charming the inner circle of career wives which she would have to join if Jon's ambitions were to be fulfilled, Ariane's head was whirling with new names and faces. Jon found her taking five minutes' break behind the marquee, wriggling her stockinged toes in the cool, dry grass.

'Are you all right, sweetheart?' he asked her mid-afternoon, ever solicitous.

'Of course,' she assured him, pushing her feet back into her high heels and reaching up to kiss his clean-shaven cheek.

She was so proud of him, so glad to see the ease with which he conducted his business. Anyone could see that Jon was set to go far and Ariane was happy to take the trip with him.

'Don't worry about me. I thought I'd go and take a look at these famous rose gardens I've been hearing about.'

Jon smiled at her, grateful for her understanding, his love clear in his eyes as he left her. Feeling warm and happy, Ariane discreetly left the crowd and made her way to the shadowy walkway which led down to the rose arbours.

It was a relief to take a breather. Her face ached from so much smiling, a dull headache pulsing behind her eyes from a surfeit of social nicety.

She gasped as she rounded a corner and unexpectedly came across the roses. Wave after wave of colour and perfume, tone on tone, stretching before her in a fragrant ocean, rippling in the gentle summer breeze.

Ariane walked down the curved stone steps and onto the emerald carpet of well-tended grass. Her high heels sank into the earth as she bent her head and breathed in the heavenly scent, closing her eyes the better to savour it.

In her mind's eye she imagined spreading a layer of petals across the bed she shared with Jon. What would it be like to sink down onto the soft, fragrant flowers? Naked skin against velvet soft petals. Snapping a rose off at the stem, she held it against her cheek, rubbing the flower against her skin.

The touch of the petals reminded her of Jon. His fingers were always gentle, his caresses skimming her senses. Knowing him as she did, she knew she could not share her harmless little fantasy with him. Making love on a blanket of rose petals would strike Jon as being mildly perverted.

It was one of the things she loved about him, his upright, straightforward nature, his unshakable confidence that he knew what was right and what was wrong. Jon's world was black and white. No shades of grey. And yet if she closed her eyes, she could see him vividly, in her mind's eye, pressing her down onto the petal-strewn sheets, their combined weight releasing the fragrance. His skin would be as velvety smooth as the petals, covering the warm steel of his muscles as he possessed her . . .

What was the matter with her lately? These brief, intensely erotic thoughts were becoming more frequent, intruding into her thoughts at the most inappropriate moments. Even when she was with Jon.

She loved him, loved the way her body responded to his loving touch. He was so careful of her, treating her as though she was made of porcelain; fragile, delicate – precious. Only sometimes . . .

'You look like an angel, surrounded by petals.'

Ariane's head shot up as the deep, unfamiliar voice sounded close to her ear. It had a slight transatlantic drawl which told her he was one of the Americans. Her cheeks suffused with embarrassed colour. The man stared at her, unsmiling, an intensity in his eyes which she found vaguely disturbing.

'I'm sorry,' she said stiltedly, 'I thought I was alone.'

'Obviously.'

His lips moved in what she supposed passed for a smile. Ariane took in his relaxed stance, the carefully casual suit and long dark hair drawn back into a ponytail. He had a narrow face with a prominent nose and firm, well-shaped lips which looked as if they didn't smile often. Overall, he looked like many of the other young, rich execs with whom she had been socialising all morning. Yet Ariane knew, with some deep intuition which she never knew she possessed, that he was different.

His scrutiny was unblinking and, although his eyes did not leave hers, she felt stripped naked before his gaze. It was almost hypnotic, making her feel breathless, unable to keep her thoughts in order.

He had unusual eyes, the pupils overly dilated, the iris no more than a thin rim of topaz. For some reason, Ariane found it difficult to tear her eyes away from them.

'I have to go,' she whispered.

'No, you don't.'

Her eyebrows shot up at his calm denial and he almost smiled properly, though not quite. She flinched, but did not pull away when his hand reached out to cup hers.

'You've hurt yourself,' he explained.

Looking down, Ariane saw that she had unknowingly crushed the stem of the rose in her palm and one of the long, vicious thorns had pierced the delicate skin. As she watched, a bright red bead of blood rose up on her white palm. Now that she had seen it, she was conscious of the pain and she grimaced.

'Allow me.'

Before she realised his intention, the stranger picked up her hand and brought it to his lips. His tongue lapped at the small wound, soothing it, leaving a shocking tremor of pleasure in its wake.

Ariane knew she should snatch back her hand, maybe even run. Instead, she heard her own voice, unrecognisably tentative, enquire, 'Who are you?'

He let go of her hand and stepped back a pace.

'What need have we of names? I don't want to know yours. From now on, I will call you Angel.'

Ariane laughed shakily.

'Forgive me if I seem rude, but I doubt that we'll meet again.'

He cocked his head slightly to one side, as if considering.

'Do you think not?'

Something about him made her want to flee, as if – ridiculous thought – there was only so much time left to her before escape would be impossible.

'I have to go.'

Walking quickly away from him, she could feel his eyes on her back. Fear, cold and undiluted, trickled down her spine, making her hurry.

Jon smiled as he saw her, taking her by the hand and introducing her to the Managing Director. As soon as he could, he drew her to one side.

'Ariane, I have to go away. It's only for six weeks, but I can't avoid it.'

Ariane could not understand the sudden panic which ricocheted through her at this news.

'Where are you going?'

'To the States – to see how they do things over there. I'd take you with me, but—'

'I couldn't,' she interrupted, afraid to hear why he didn't want her to go. 'I mean, I'm just beginning to build up my client list, I couldn't afford to go away now.'

Was it her imagination, or did his smile hold an element of relief?

'It won't seem like so long, darling, you'll see. It's a promotion. When I get back, we'll be able to start planning our wedding.'

He pulled her into his arms as if he didn't want to see the uncertainty in her eyes. Over his shoulder Ariane saw the stranger emerge from the rose garden. To her horror, he headed straight towards them.

'Jon! Jon, there's a man . . .'

'Jon – how are you?'

To Ariane's discomfort, the man shook her fiancé's hand, greeting him like an old friend. Inevitably he turned his eyes questioningly towards Ariane, his smile deceptively genial.

'Darling, this is Luke Conrad, my counterpart at the American office. He'll be taking my place here while I'm at his desk in New York,'

Jon smiled as if there was a satisfying symmetry to the arrangement, unaware of the irrational alarm it had triggered in Ariane. Conrad took her reluctantly proffered hand and she winced as his palm pressed against the small wound made by the rose thorn. Jon was instantly solicitous.

'What is it, darling?'

Ariane felt the hot colour flood her cheeks.

'It . . . it's nothing . . .'

Her eyes clashed with Conrad's and she was conscious that she was pleading with him not to mention their encounter in the rose garden to Jon. She had to force herself to concentrate on what Jon was saying.

'I'm so glad you two have met today, Ariane is unhappy about my being away. The company she was working for went into liquidation recently, so she's got too much time on her hands. Coming so soon after her parents died . . . I think I told you about the accident?'

The man inclined his head slightly in assent, and Ariane noticed he didn't bother to try to offer a polite condolence, preferring instead to keep silent. She was glad. It was bad enough that he seemed to know so much about her, she didn't want any empty expressions of sympathy.

'I do have my freelance work,' she protested softly, aware that Jon had made her sound quite useless.

'Ariane is an illustrator.'

Jon smiled indulgently at her, sending a surge of irritation through her veins. Her mouth fell open in horror at his next words.

'You must come and have dinner with us before I leave – would tomorrow suit you?'

'That's very kind – if that's all right with you?' Conrad turned to Ariane, his tone solicitous, though his eyes challenged her.

Ariane felt trapped. She had no reason to be reluctant to have this man in her home, and to retract Jon's invitation would be inexcusably rude. Yet she didn't want him to come. Worse, she had the feeling that Luke Conrad knew this and was amused by her dilemma.

'Of course,' she replied coolly, 'I shall look forward to it.'

'Liar!'

Ariane's eyes widened as she saw his lips form the word, sure for a moment that he had actually spoken aloud. But no, he couldn't have. Jon hadn't heard him. As if from far away, she heard the two men make polite noises of farewell, and then Conrad was walking away.

Later, Ariane lay passive as Jon moved inside her, his lips and fingers gentle on her breast. A swift, shocking picture pushed its way into her mind, of Conrad's dark head against her breast instead of Jon's familiar blond one.

*His* lips wouldn't be tender, they would bruise and nip; take, rather than coax the pleasure from her. Closing her eyes against Jon's loving face, Ariane imagined it was Conrad driving into her body, saw herself raising up her hips to meet him, thrust for thrust, her nails raking down his back as he battered against her womb . . . she came, violently, precipitating Jon's orgasm.

'Darling, that was wonderful,' he whispered to her in the darkness.

Ariane squeezed her eyes shut tightly, containing her shame.

Conrad brought her flowers when he arrived for dinner. White roses. Ariane forced herself to smile, arranging them in a glass vase and placing them defiantly at the centre of the table as if to show him she didn't remember their significance.

All afternoon she had cooked and prepared for this dinner, determined to treat it in the same way as every other business meal she had ever hosted for Jon. The men talked shop over tender spring lamb and soft red wine while Ariane concentrated on maintaining a normal heart rate.

What was it about this man that disturbed her so much? Tonight he was dressed all in black – black trousers, black silk shirt open at the neck to reveal a glimpse of black chest hair against bronzed skin. His hair was loose, parted in the middle and falling in a glossy, wavy curtain to his collarbones.

To Jon, he was congenial enough. Even when he spoke to Ariane, his words were invariably polite, and proper. Yet all the while his eyes mocked her, challenged her to – what? What was it he expected from her?

After dinner, Jon went to fetch more wine and Ariane was left alone with him in the living room.

'You seem nervous, Angel,' he said softly.

'Don't call me that,' she snapped quickly.

He smiled.

'That's better.'

'What?'

'You've been so polite all evening. I was beginning to feel quite offended.'

He was standing very close, looking down on her from his additional four or five inches, his expression intent. Ariane could feel the warmth of his body through the thin silk of his shirt, reaching out to her. Her mouth and throat ran dry and she swayed very slightly towards him.

Conrad's eyes settled on her parted lips and his eyelids dropped to half cover his eyes, shielding his expression. He raised his hand, extending his forefinger a little and for a moment she thought that he was going to touch her. Then he smiled and his hand dropped down to his side, just as Jon reappeared with the wine.

Shielded by Jon's jovial bonhomie, Ariane went to sit in an armchair, conscious of the heavy pulse of desire in the pit of her stomach. Her hand trembled as she took her glass and he frowned at her as a little of the wine slopped over the side and ran down her fingers. Without thinking, she licked the spillage from her skin.

Feeling Conrad's eyes on her, she blushed deeply, and pressed herself further into her seat. From then on she wanted nothing more than for the evening to be over, for him to go.

When, at last, the time came, Ariane went with Jon to the front door of the flat.

'Feel free to call by any time while I'm away – Ariane is here most of the day, aren't you, darling?'

'I . . . perhaps if you could phone first,' she replied faintly, trying to ignore Jon's look of surprise.

'Of course. I wouldn't want to interrupt your work. Thank you for such a lovely meal. You must allow me to take you out to dinner one evening to repay you.'

'That won't be necessary.'

'Ariane! Thank you, Conrad. I'm sure Ariane might be glad of some company while I'm away.'

Conrad inclined his head slightly before turning away, though not before Ariane had seen his smile.

'Why did you do that?' she rounded on Jon as soon as he closed the door.

Jon's eyebrows shot up in surprise at her tone.

'I worry about you, sweetheart.'

'I can take care of myself. I don't like that man.'

9

Jon looked bewildered by her vehemence.

'I don't see how you can say that on such a short acquaintance. What's the matter with you? You've been acting strangely all evening.'

'I told you. I don't like him.' Ariane heard her own voice rise on a note of irritation. Jon was instantly contrite, taking her in his arms and smoothing her hair.

'I'm sorry, darling, I didn't mean to sound so patronising! Look, if you feel that strongly about it, I'll ask Conrad to send his secretary if anything needs collecting from here.'

'Won't that seem odd?' she asked, feeling ashamed.

'It doesn't matter. So long as you're happy.'

'I love you,' she whispered.

Jon laughed and kissed her on the nose.

'I love you too, sweetheart.'

He arrived on her doorstep the afternoon after Jon left.

'What are you doing here?' she said baldly.

She had forgotten how attractive he was. Wearing a blue denim shirt tucked loosely into slightly darker jeans, his physical presence alone reached out to her, engulfing her.

'Hello, Angel,' he said, his smile designed to infuriate her.

'Didn't Jon tell you I didn't want you to come?'

'Yes.'

'Then why are you here now?'

He smiled slowly.

'To fuck you. The rest is up to you.'

Ariane blinked. The breath hurt in her chest, her heart hammering so hard she felt it could burst out of her ribcage. The blood sang in her ears as she stared at him.

God, she wanted him so badly! A pulse beat insistently

between her legs as she stared at him, making a mockery of her claims to dislike him. She didn't *need* to like him, the attraction between them was purely physical. Perhaps that was what had frightened her from the moment they met.

He made no move to push his way inside the flat, he just stood there staring calmly at her, waiting for Ariane to make the decision. As if in a fugue, Ariane stepped aside and let him in.

He waited until she had closed the front door of the flat. Turning, she bumped against him, taken by surprise by his nearness.

'Oh!' she gasped, bringing her hands up automatically to steady herself. Conrad caught her hands in his and pressed her palms against his chest. She could feel the steady thump of his heart through the fabric and the heat of his skin seemed to sear her fingers. He stopped her from pulling away, his eyes staring deeply into hers, drinking in the confusion, and the desire, which Ariane knew they expressed.

His lips curved slightly and he brought her hands up to his mouth. Without breaking eye contact, he kissed each knuckle in turn. His lips were dry and soft, warm against her skin. Ariane shivered, conscious of their touch even as he moved from knuckle to knuckle. There was a strange, sinking feeling in the pit of her stomach which made her legs feel weak. Her head was spinning, her resistance slipping away like quicksilver.

Something about his confidence, his absolute conviction that she wanted him was arousing her beyond anything she had ever known before. His words in the rose garden flashed into her mind – *what need have we of names* – and for the first time, she understood what he had meant. She didn't want to know him, didn't need to love him. The desire she felt was purely physical, an overwhelming, animal urge which only he could assuage.

11

Ariane felt her eyelids droop as if weighted and her head fell back. She swayed slightly towards him and he let go of one of her hands so that he could slip one hand behind her head, supporting her at the nape of her neck.

He didn't say a word, though his eyes bored into hers, as if reading her every thought. A sigh trembled across Ariane's lower lip and, at last, his gaze moved from her eyes to her lips. She imagined she could feel that regard caressing the sensitive skin of her inner lips and she trembled, willing him to kiss her even as she dreaded it.

Pressing her closer, Conrad trapped her palm between them whilst he linked the fingers of his free hand with hers and drew her arm up, over her shoulder. Ariane felt the hard, cool surface of the wall against her back as he leaned into her. Her fingers clutched at his as he lowered his head, so slowly, to hers.

'No!' The word, small and unconvincing, whispered through her lips, brushing against his.

'No?'

She could feel the heat of his body enclosing her, the potent thrust of his erection pressing against the softness of her lower belly. At every point of contact with his, her body seemed to burn with a restless desire. He was looking at her again, his gaze mesmerising as his lips brushed, feather-light, across the surface of hers. Ariane felt as though the touch was electrically charged and she pouted instinctively, yearning for him to kiss her properly. Her lips ached for him, every last vestige of control slipping away inexorably.

'No?' he repeated softly, the small word reverberating with teasing mockery.

Ariane realised, then, that he was waiting for her to say yes. That, ultimately, the choice was hers. Until that moment, the fear of him that she had experienced in the rose garden had remained, holding her back. Instinctively, she knew that, if she said no again, he would leave. It would be over. But if she said yes . . .

'Yes,' she whispered, her voice no more than a breath. His lips were unexpectedly gentle as they moved against hers. She had expected him to be thrusting, forceful, even violent. Instead, he nibbled and licked at her lips, teasing and coaxing until her mouth opened eagerly, granting him access to the hot, sweet recesses within.

Ariane whimpered, deep in her throat and clutched at the fabric of his shirt as the kiss deepened and his tongue probed at hers. She felt as if she was turning to liquid, melting against him. As he moved his mouth away from hers, she drew in a ragged breath. His lips touched the fragile, exposed skin of her wrist. Holding her arm up, pressed against the wall, he blazed a trail of kisses along its underside, nuzzling at its junction with her shoulder and moving across the delicate sweep of her collarbones.

At the tender dip between them, he dabbed the very tip of his tongue against her skin. It was such a delicate caress, yet it sent ripples of pleasure through her, causing her breasts to swell and harden, the nipples cresting wantonly, pressing against the inadequate, lacy confinement of her bra.

'Oh . . . please!' she gasped as he moved his head across her breast, breathing warmly on the thin fabric of her blouse, teasing her.

He looked up at her and, holding her eye, blew gently on her nipple.

'Please – what?' he said quietly. Ariane looked down at him with a kind of confused desperation. Her arm was aching as he held it up, yet she was aware that he was holding it in such a way that her right breast was thrown into sharp relief, making it deliciously vulnerable to his caresses. She didn't understand what he wanted from her.

'Luke . . . ? Please . . . ?'

His lips twitched slightly.

'What is it you want me to do?' he asked her patiently.

He gazed steadily at her as her eyes widened with dismay. Surely he didn't want her to say aloud how much she wanted him? Ariane's mind rebelled as she realised that, more, he wanted her to verbalise exactly what she wanted him to do to her. And she knew that she couldn't do it.

'I . . . I can't!' she whispered, her face contorting with anguish. Why didn't he just undo her blouse and use his mouth to ease the ache in her nipple? Didn't he want to suck and lick her, to flick his tongue across the hot, burgeoning peak . . . ?

His eyes challenged her and Ariane knew that he was aware of the conflict going through her mind. And with a sudden flash of insight, she realised too that he was turned on by her anguish. Ultimately, his desire for her would feed on her capitulation to his demands.

Now he regarded her almost quizzically, his head on one side. Slowly, he straightened. Ariane moaned slightly, aware that for the moment she had lost the chance of having her breast enclosed in the heat of his clever mouth.

'What can't you do, Angel?' he asked her, no trace of his arousal in his voice.

'I . . . I can't . . . talk about it,' she admitted.

He let go of her arm and cupped her face with both his hands. Though he had released it, Ariane did not move her arm. She was conscious of the steely length of his body pressing into the softness of hers, of the size of his erection, undiminished in spite of her reluctance.

'Let me help you,' he said, his voice low and soft, trickling across her senses like a soothing balm. 'You want me to undress you, to touch your skin with my fingers and my lips . . . you want my mouth at your breasts, Angel, don't you?'

'Yes,' she admitted, her voice cracking with need.

'Then tell me.'

There was a hint of steel in his voice now and Ariane closed her eyes momentarily against the intensity of his gaze.

'I don't know what to say.'

'Say – suck my tits, Conrad.'

Ariane's eyes flew open in shock at the crudity of his words. He smiled at her shock, his topaz eyes glittering with some unfathomable emotion.

'I can't!' she protested weakly,

Conrad shrugged and moved away from her slightly, just enough for her to feel the chill between them.

'Of course you can. If you won't, then I shall go.'

She didn't want him to go. Somewhere in the back of her mind, where rationality still held sway, Ariane realised he had timed this exactly so that she was too far gone not to give in. He knew that she could not bear for him to walk away now, that he had already taken her too far. She swallowed hard. When she spoke, her voice sounded alien to her, as if it was coming from far away.

'Please, Conrad – suck my tits.'

She gasped as he pulled her blouse apart and cupped her breasts in his palms. With his thumbs, he pushed the lacy cups aside so that the two rosy, puckered areolae were exposed. Ariane cried aloud as he dipped his head and drew one aching peak into his mouth.

The gentleness was gone now, in its place was a hunger that matched her own, a need which drew her still further away from the reality of what she was doing. As he drew on her nipple, suckling like a baby at the breast, Ariane felt an answering pull deep in her womb. Between her legs, the flesh swelled and moistened and her clitoris began to pulse. She was dangerously close to climax already.

Vaguely, she was aware that they were sliding together down the wall. She clung to his shoulders as they sank onto the serviceable hall carpet, Conrad's mouth still clamped to her breast. His hand pushed under the hem of her skirt and made contact with the damp gusset of her briefs. He sighed against her breast.

'Ohh!' Ariane wriggled her hips against the hard floor as he insinuated his fingers beneath the elastic of her briefs and pulled them to one side.

Raising his head from her breast, he watched her face as he sank his fingers gently into the satiny cleft of her sex, his fingertips unerringly finding the hard button of her clitoris.

'Is this what you want?' he breathed raggedly.

There was no inner debate this time, Ariane gasped and said, 'Yes, oh yes!'

Ariane reached for the telltale bulge in his jeans, but he caught hold of her fingers and pressed them instead between her own legs.

'Feel how hot you are,' he told her, his eyes devouring her face. 'How wet.'

Under pressure from his fingers, Ariane felt her fingertips enter her own body as Conrad tapped sharply against her clitoris. She cried out as the unexpected movement tipped her into orgasm.

'Oh God! ' she cried, pulling her hands away and reaching for him. 'Fuck me now – please, please, fuck me!'

For the first time since she had met him, Conrad smiled.

'Not this time, Angel,' he said.

It took a few minutes for his words to penetrate the fog of Ariane's mind. Even when the shock of them hit her, she didn't believe him. How could he not want her after what had just happened? She knew that he was aroused – his erection was clearly visible, pressing against the front of his jeans so hard that she knew he must be uncomfortable. She clutched at his buttocks, trying to pull him against her, but he covered her hands with his and disengaged them gently.

Ariane felt hot colour suffuse her cheeks as she realised that he was serious. She felt humiliated, embarrassed by her own need.

'Conrad—'

'Ssh!'

His eyes raked her face, and Ariane knew that he would see that she was dazed, still not quite back on earth. Without a word, he readjusted her panties and pulled down her skirt. Holding out his hand to her, he helped her to her feet.

Ariane realised that she was shaking and, slowly, anger replaced her humiliation. How dare he treat her like this? Conrad watched the change come over her face without comment. He seemed . . . *satisfied*, as if she had passed some kind of a test.

Reaching for her, he cupped her cheek in his palm and kissed her, hard, on the lips.

'Goodbye, Angel,' he said.

Before she realised his intention, he was out of the door, leaving her listening in a daze to his footsteps as they ran down the stairs. As he reached the outer door, fury galvanised her into action.

Flying over to the living-room window, she threw it wide and leaned out. She could see him across the street, climbing into a black Porsche.

'Bastard!' she shouted as he gunned the engine, drowning out her outrage.

# Two

The roses arrived that evening. Pure white roses, the petals glistening with a fine film of moisture. Perfect.

*For my Angel – until next time.*

Ariane let the card fall to the floor. Her heart seemed to flutter in her chest like a butterfly caught in cupped hands. Her breathing faltered and she buried her face in the roses, inhaling their scent deeply.

What had happened to her? Like a wild animal she had rolled on the floor with Conrad, trying to pull him into her with a feverish desire which bordered on desperation. Never had she felt such a need, such an overwhelming impulse to fuck and be fucked. For that was all it was, she had no illusions to the contrary. She had wanted him purely as a means of self-gratification and she wasn't proud of the memory.

Oh Lord, what had she done? Closing her eyes, she held the bouquet against her breasts, the events of the afternoon replaying across her closed eyelids. *Until next time.* The words were scorched across her mind and she repeated them like a mantra, knowing that, for all her self-revulsion, she wanted there to be a next time, and soon. Please let it be soon!

Jon phoned later, in the evening. She was lying on the sofa, trying to read a magazine but her eyes kept straying to the roses, now arranged in a vase in the middle of the coffee table. She almost knocked them over as she reached, reflexively, for the phone.

'Ariane? How are you?'

'Oh, Jon! It's lovely to hear your voice!' she said instinctively, sure that his call would be her salvation. 'How are you?'

'Fine. Have you seen much of Luke Conrad?'

The question, coming out of the blue like that, took Ariane by surprise. She was glad Jon couldn't see her across the miles, for she was sure that the blood had drained out of her face and that the expression in her eyes as she thought of what had happened would instantly give her away.

'No, not really. He called by briefly this afternoon.' She winced at her own economy with the truth, but Jon seemed oblivious.

'Great. I was met at the airport by Luke's fiancé, Melissa. It was thoughtful of him to get her to meet me, don't you think?'

'What's she like?'

'Tall, brunette, willowy—'

'I didn't mean what does she *look* like,' Ariane interrupted him impatiently. Then: 'Is she very lovely?' she asked.

Jon's soft chuckle transcended the distance between them with ease.

'Very. Almost as lovely as you. I miss you, Ariane.'

'I miss you, too,' she replied truthfully. 'Will you phone again tomorrow?'

'I'll try. Sleep well, sweetheart.'

'I will. Goodbye, Jon.'

She held the receiver close to her for a moment after the dialling tone began. If only Jon hadn't had to go away, if only he was here with her now, none of this would have happened.

*It was waiting to happen*, a rogue voice mocked her in her

head. *You've been waiting for this forever.*

'No!' she whispered, reaching out to finger the velvet-soft petals of the roses. She wouldn't see Conrad again – she would forget the feeling that had flared between them. Jon would come back and everything would be the same as before; it would be as if this brief, fleeting moment of madness had never happened.

She woke to the sound of the telephone ringing beside the bed. Groggy with sleep, she groped for it, expecting to hear Jon's familiar voice again.

'Darling?'

'Good morning, Angel. Your greeting warms my heart!'

Ariane recoiled from the deep, mocking voice on the other end of the telephone.

'What do *you* want?' she said bluntly, rubbing her hand across her eyes to dispel the blurry remnants of sleep.

'You know what I want, Angel.'

Ariane felt her blood slow and thicken, as if warm honey was trickling through her veins. How could he reach out to her like this, his disembodied voice curling round her senses so that she could hardly think straight?

'Please leave me alone,' she said, aware that her voice lacked conviction.

Conrad laughed softly.

'I can't do that, Angel. Now I've helped you to see your reflection, it would be cruel to deny you access to the mirror.'

'My reflection?'

'Of your inner self. Think of me as the mirror in which you can see yourself, Angel. Think of me as reflecting your deepest, darkest desires.'

Ariane swallowed. Her mouth and throat had grown dry as

his words had rolled through her mind. She barely heard what he said, it was his tone, the way he spoke that captivated her. His voice was like music, his phraseology like poetry, coating her senses.

'Are you still in bed, Angel?'

'Yes,' she whispered.

'Lie back on the pillows – relax, Are you comfortable?'

Ariane settled into the pillows at her back and turned her head to one side so that the telephone receiver was trapped against her ear.

'Yes, I'm comfortable now,' she replied. 'Where are you?'

'Shh – don't speak. Only respond to what I say to you. Do you understand?'

She frowned, conscious of the note of command in his tone which, in other circumstances, she would find unacceptable. Nevertheless, she found herself answering.

'I understand.'

'Good.' His voice softened again and Ariane relaxed, unaware, until then, that she was tracking his mood, subconsciously seeking his approval. 'I've been thinking of you, Angel. All night I've been thinking of you. Remembering the way you look, the way you taste, the perfume of your skin . . .'

'Don't . . .' she whispered half-heartedly, aware that his words were arousing her, that the heat of need was building in the pit of her stomach once more. Conrad ignored her, continuing as if she had never spoken.

'. . . if I close my eyes I can see you now. You're lying on your bed . . . under the sheets. What colour are your sheets, Angel?'

'Blue,' she whispered, glancing down at the smart new bedlinen she and Jon had chosen together.

'They should be white. I'll send you some. What are you wearing, Angel?'

'My – my nightdress.'

'Describe it to me.'

'It's pink . . . with roses . . .'

'How sweet! Does it have sleeves?'

'No, it has thin straps and a shaped bodice—'

'With buttons at the front?'

'Yes . . .'

'Is it tight across your breasts?'

Glancing down, Ariane realised that, though it had fitted her perfectly well before, now the fabric was straining across her breasts which had swollen in response to Conrad's seductive voice.

'It *is* tight,' she admitted.

'Unfasten the buttons, Angel,' he told her.

Biting her lip, Ariane did as he asked, a small sigh escaping her as the pressure on her aching breasts was instantly relieved. Conrad heard it and Ariane could sense the smile in his voice as he spoke again.

'That's better, isn't it? Are you hot, Angel?'

'Yes.'

'Touch your arms . . . stroke your fingertips down to your elbows . . . is your skin warm?'

'Yes . . .'

'Damp, even?'

'No, not damp . . . but my fingers slip easily across my skin . . .'

'Good girl. Is it pleasant, stroking your arms?'

'Mmm,' she replied, barely aware that she continued to caress herself, so lightly, making the small, fine hairs stand up on the surface of her skin.

'Touch your breasts . . . feel how soft the skin is between them . . .'

Ariane did as he said, aware of the arousal churning through her veins.

'Yes.'

'Touch them with the very tips of your fingers . . . is that good, Angel?'

'Mmm.'

'I can hear it is. Press them, Angel, make them lie flat against your breasts . . . I can tell by the sound of your breathing that you have obeyed me. You will obey me, won't you, Angel?'

Ariane murmured, enjoying herself too much to protest, yet conscious that the word *obey* was not one with which she felt comfortable.

'You must obey – if you don't make your promise I shall hang up here and now and you'll never hear from me again.'

His cold, clipped words sent ripples of panic running through Ariane's body.

'I will! I will obey you, Conrad . . . please don't go!'

There was silence for a few minutes.

'Prove it,' he said at last.

Ariane's voice was full of anguish.

'How?' she whispered.

'Squeeze your nipples between your thumbs and forefingers.'

Ariane moved her fingers to comply.

'Harder – hard enough for it to hurt.'

She gasped as the pressure increased to the point of discomfort.

'Harder.'

'I . . . I can't!'

'You can, my Angel. You can squeeze those hard little pips until tears spring to your eyes. Do it, Angel. Do it for me.'

Ariane squeezed until her heart began to pump faster in response to the little messages of pain radiating out from her compressed nipples.

'Does it hurt, Angel?' His voice was low and silky in her ear.

'Yes,' she whispered, her face screwed up with effort.

'Pull them, Angel, and twist.'

'Oh . . . oh, please . . . let me stop! It hurts!'

There was a pause, then he said, 'Very well, you may let go now.'

Ariane cried out as her nipples sprung back to their normal position.

'Describe to me how they feel, Angel,' he demanded.

'They burn,' she said, rubbing her palms over the abused flesh.

'Good. Now touch yourself between your legs – see how much you enjoyed the pain.'

'Oh God!' she breathed as she felt the heavy, viscous seepage which gave her away.

Sinking her fingers into the slippery channels of flesh, she felt the pain in her nipples mellow to an ache that was strangely pleasurable. Breasts and womb seemed linked by an invisible cord that vibrated with longing.

'Are you wet, my Angel? Does your cunt weep with shame?'

'Yes,' she said, her voice thin and high-pitched. 'Help me, Conrad . . . !'

He chuckled softly.

'I can just see you, legs apart and breasts spilling out of your nightdress, like a fallen angel with your hands between your legs. Can you feel an echo of yesterday afternoon's climax, Angel?'

Realising that she could, Ariane whispered, 'Yes . . .'

'Are you frigging yourself?'

'Yes – oh yes!' She was breathless, panting as her fingers strummed her straining clitoris.

'Stop at once!'

'But—'

'Stop!'

'Oh!'

Ariane brought her hands up, closing her eyes against the frustration. Conrad was speaking again, his words measured, his tone brooking no argument.

'I am master of your pleasure now, Angel. You will not come without my permission, your body is not yours to stimulate at will. Do you understand me?'

'Yes,' she whispered.

'Good. Now – you may touch your clit with your forefinger. Very lightly.'

He waited until her broken sigh told him that she had complied.

'Does that feel good?'

'Mmm.'

'Stroke it, very gently. Round and round . . .'

Ariane sighed as her senses heightened, aware that if she continued she would soon reach a climax. Conrad's next words shocked and dismayed her. 'Now smack it, Angel. Tap your finger against that hard little nub. Are you doing it?' he asked harshly.

'Yes,' she gasped, drumming her fingertip against the flesh that had so enjoyed the light caress of her fingertip only minutes before. 'But . . . it hurts!'

'Of course it hurts!' He sounded scornful and Ariane recoiled from his tone. 'Have you learned nothing yet? Tap harder – beat it . . . I can hear you panting, Angel. Spread your legs wider while you abuse yourself.'

Ariane obeyed him blindly, her forefinger tapping relentlessly at her clitoris, her hips bucking as her climax was released.

'Oh, dear God!' she cried as she came, mashing her fingers against the bud which convulsed against them.

Only as the first violent wave of pleasure subsided did she realise that there was an ominous silence at the other end of the telephone.

'Conrad?' she whispered, afraid that he had hung up.

'You came without permission,' he said, his voice cold and hard.

Ariane felt a trickle of apprehension run along her spine.

'I . . . I'm sorry,' she said, her voice small. Drawing her knees up to her chin, she hugged them close in a protective gesture that did little to calm the sudden pounding of her heart.

'You *will* be sorry, Angel,' Conrad promised her silkily. 'Very sorry. You'll be hearing from me soon. Be ready.'

The telephone clicked, leaving Ariane with the dialling tone buzzing in her ear.

Jon picked up the telephone to call Ariane, then realised that it was early morning in England and she would probably still be asleep. He missed her, and she had sounded odd when they had spoken the night before.

'You're looking worried!'

He looked up as Melissa walked through the open office door, brightening as he saw her. It had been a pleasant surprise to find that Luke Conrad's girlfriend worked with him – after she had met him at the airport he had come to regard her as a friendly face amongst all his new colleagues.

'I was just thinking about Ariane,' he admitted as she sat down. 'She sounded a bit . . . well, unlike herself, I suppose, when I spoke to her last night. I hope she's coping on her own.'

Melissa raised a finely plucked eyebrow.

'It sounds as if she's very needy,' she commented.

Grimacing, Jon shook his head.

'I didn't mean to make her sound spineless or anything. Don't think that Ariane is a clinging vine, far from it! It's just that this is the first time we've been apart since her parents were killed and she's come to depend on me.'

'And you like that – the fact that she *depends* on you?'

Jon looked at her, feeling mildly taken aback.

'I've never really thought about it, to be honest, but yes, I suppose I do like it.'

Melissa smiled and he noticed, not for the first time, that she had the whitest, most brace-perfect teeth he had ever encountered.

'You obviously have a very strong protective streak. A lot of women find that very attractive in a man.'

Jon held her eye and wondered, not for the first time, if she was flirting with him. What would he do if she was? He'd barely glanced at other women since he and Ariane had started living together, but Melissa was something else. She was almost as tall as he was, but so slender that she gave an impression of vulnerability which drew him to her. Her hair was long and straight, falling in a glossy brown curtain from a centre parting, and her eyes were a soft, moist brown that missed nothing.

Then she grinned and the moment passed.

'Luke will look out for Ariane, I shouldn't worry if I were you. I brought you the report you wanted to look at before the meeting,' she told him, businesslike now. 'I'd pay special attention to section twelve, if I were you. Especially paragraph three B.'

'Thanks!' Jon grinned at her, resolutely keeping his eyes averted from the alluring roll of her hips as she walked across the room.

'I was wondering,' she said, turning as she reached the door. 'It can be pretty lonely in a strange town all on your own. Maybe you'd like to go see a movie one night?'

Jon felt his heart lift.

'Thanks, Melissa, that would be great.'

'Tonight?'

He shrugged.

'Why not?'

What harm could it do? he asked himself as he was left alone. He was only keeping Melissa company while Conrad was away, just as Conrad was keeping an eye on Ariane for him. What could be neater?

Ariane found herself waiting for Conrad's retribution with an increasing sense of anxiety. What had he meant, she would be sorry? In the cold light of day, the hazy sensuality of the morning seemed very far away, and Conrad's threats seemed vaguely ridiculous.

Ariane worked doggedly at her drawing board, trying to sustain her interest in the cartoon character she was supposed to be working on. All the while she was aware that she kept an ear half cocked for the telephone, or the knock on the door that would tell her he had arrived.

Of course, he had to work, too, she told herself as she picked at a salad at lunch time. What was the matter with her? He had promised her retribution for her perceived disobedience, and she was awaiting it as eagerly as if he had promised her a treat!

When there was a knock at the door mid-afternoon, Ariane's pulse seemed to mark double time as she went, on trembling legs to open it. She almost sagged with disappointment when she saw the courier outside.

'Miss Angel?' he said.

Ariane nodded wordlessly.

'Sign here, please – I have a parcel for you.'

The parcel was large and cumbersome and Ariane staggered with it to the bedroom where she laid it on the bed. Inside there were pure white, Egyptian cotton sheets and pillowcases and a small parcel on which he had written:

*'Wear the enclosed and come to Room 29 of the Grantham Hotel at seven'*

That was it. No personal greeting or kind word, just a command, to be obeyed, or ignored at her peril. His writing was large and bold, as authoritative as the man himself.

Trembling, Ariane opened the second box. Inside, there was a white blouse in a layered, diaphanous fabric which was soft to the touch. With it was a red, flippy skirt, so short that it would barely cover the crease between her legs and her buttocks. A pair of briefs, black and thong-backed completed the ensemble, together with a pair of black patent leather stiletto-heeled mules.

In the bottom of the box was another note.

*'Paint your finger and toe-nails scarlet and wear matching lipstick. Do not wear mascara – you will be shedding tears tonight. No tights and no bra.'*

To her shame, Ariane almost came just reading the words. There was something so intensely erotic about being told what to wear, where to go. To be dressed by a man purely for sex. But she couldn't understand her excitement at the promise of pain.

She spent the rest of the day in a state of nervous tension, waiting for the time to come when she could change and set off. It was useless to even try to work, the pictures she was trying to create were constantly obscured by other, cruder images which distracted her. Absently, she made a series of sketches of a woman, dressed the way she would be dressed tonight, her face contorted by bliss . . . or by tears. Why tears? What was he planning to do to her?

Briefly, it crossed Ariane's mind that Conrad could be deranged, that she was foolish to go along with the game he was playing with her. But that was it, the crux of the matter – she knew it to be no more than a game. No matter what he said, or she came to feel, the fact was that he had given her several opportunities to call a halt, both last night and this morning, but she had chosen not to.

She could walk away at any time, he wouldn't try to stop her. Even as she thought it, Ariane knew that, even so, she wouldn't. He had her hooked, like a junkie needing a fix, he had given her just enough to make her crave for more.

The sheets Conrad had sent felt crisp, yet soft as she put them on the bed. How curious that he wanted control, even in this, the colour of her sheets! More curious still was the fact that she had immediately stripped the usual bedding away and replaced it with Conrad's choice, she told herself ruefully.

She couldn't explain it, even to herself. It was as if meeting Conrad had triggered a train of events which, once begun, was unstoppable.

She started to get ready at five. First she soaked in a deep, fragrant bath before washing her hair and cleansing her face. Applying her make-up afterwards, she stared into her own over-bright eyes and wondered at the buzz of excitement already travelling through her veins. As instructed, she painted her finger and toe-nails with bright red varnish before drying her hair into a fluffy blonde cloud around her face.

The skirt and blouse were at least one size too small and she had to wriggle her way into them. Seeing how her bare nipples pressed conspicuously against the diaphanous fabric of the blouse, Ariane took it off again and put on a white bra first. Surely Conrad would not expect her to go out in public thus exposed?

Gazing at herself in the mirror afterwards, she realised she looked like a cheap tart. Her sex was just covered at the front by the wispy briefs, but the thong back meant that her buttocks were fully exposed beneath the inadequate fabric of the skirt. As she drove to the Grantham Hotel, she was conscious of her bare buttocks and thighs rubbing uncomfortably against the itchy fabric of the car seat. Parking the car, she climbed out and teetered across the car park on the unaccustomed high heels.

Crossing the wide, carpeted foyer of the hotel, Ariane felt horribly conspicuous in her tarty outfit. She didn't blame the receptionist for eyeing her with some distaste, and it took all her courage to walk calmly past the desk on her way to the lifts. Half expecting to be challenged, she breathed a sigh of relief when the lift doors closed and she was transported, alone, to the second floor.

Conrad opened the door on her second knock. He was barefoot, wearing black denim jeans and a black shirt, open at the neck. He didn't return her smile, and his eyes were hard as he travelled over her from head to toe.

'Hello,' she said, giving him a nervous smile.

Conrad frowned, and she wondered if she was even supposed to wait until he gave her permission to speak. Whatever it was, he was obviously displeased with her for some reason. Ariane could feel her heart thudding in her chest as she walked past him into the hotel room.

She found herself in the living area of a three-room suite. There was a sofa and an armchair arranged around a coffee table, on which sat a huge bowl of fruit. A television flickered, in the corner of the room, the sound turned to a low murmur, but Conrad made no attempt to switch it off. Nor did he invite her to sit down and Ariane eyed him uncertainly, sensing that she had angered him, yet not sure how.

'Do you like the outfit?' she asked him nervously, turning slowly so that he could see her from all angles.

'You disobeyed me.'

His voice was cold and flat and Ariane felt the goosebumps rise up on her skin.

'I . . . I don't think so,' she protested, her voice very small. 'I followed your instructions . . .' her stomach plummeted as she realised he was staring at her blouse. 'I . . . I couldn't come out without a bra, Conrad, I—'

'*Couldn't*?' he interrupted her. 'Or *wouldn't*?'

'It looked obscene . . . I felt too uncomfortable – oh!'

He moved across the room at lightening speed and curled his fingers in the hair at the back of her neck. Applying just enough pressure to bend her head back without hurting her, he forced her to look into his eyes.

'You use this word "I" too much, Angel. Haven't you got it yet? There is no "I" for you while you are with me. You don't need to think, or worry – you can trust me to tell you what is right for you.' He smiled, a thin, cruel smile that Ariane did not trust. 'Now you will go into the bathroom, and you will come out dressed as I instructed you to dress.'

He let her go and Ariane obeyed him immediately. In the sanctuary of the bathroom, she unbuttoned the blouse and took off the bra before putting the blouse back on. For a moment she gazed at her reflection in the mirrored wall. Her breasts were heaving under the thin fabric of the blouse, the areolae showing pink through the white material. Her bare legs looked terribly vulnerable beneath the ultra-short skirt, the shiny black patent leather of her mules reflecting the light from the bulb overhead.

Suddenly, it occurred to her that Conrad might be even more angry if she lingered too long in the bathroom, and she hurried out, finding him sprawled on the sofa, watching the television. He glanced up at her, his eyes laser-sharp as they passed across her blouse, and she stood awkwardly in front of him, waiting for him to speak.

After a moment, he looked at her again, as if wondering why she was there.

'Shall I sit down?' she suggested.

'No. I want to look at you.'

Ariane stood, feeling horribly self-conscious in the tarty outfit as he ran his eyes slowly over her, lingering on her semi-naked breasts and the shadowed apex of her thighs. After a moment, he made a circling movement with his forefinger, and she turned around.

She imagined she could feel his eyes boring into her, caressing the slope of her buttocks and running down the backs of her legs. Ariane had never been . . . *examined* – there was no other word for it – quite so thoroughly before. After a few minutes, to her intense discomfort, she realised that she was growing warm, her body was responding to such an overtly sexual gaze with pleasure rather than embarrassment.

Just as that realisation hit her, Conrad broke into her thoughts.

'Turn to face me again,' he said, his voice like dark treacle.

Ariane knew at once that he knew how she felt. His expression was inscrutable as he gazed at her, but there was something so knowing about his eyes that she realised that she could keep no secrets from him. One look at her and he could divine her every thought, her every desire, even the most shameful. *Especially* the most shameful.

'Now,' he said, steepling his fingers together and tapping them thoughtfully against his chin, 'what are we to do with you?'

Ariane's mouth ran dry as she stared at him, waiting for him to continue. Her stomach churned with a mixture of apprehension and excitement, a combination that thrilled and appalled her in equal measure.

Conrad rose and she watched him warily as he approached her. Holding herself absolutely still, Ariane sought to control the inconvenient trembling of her limbs as he stroked her hair. It was such a tender gesture, almost loving. Ariane swallowed, hard, aware that his touch was deceptive. He was playing with her, teasing her like a cat with a mouse, trying to lull her into a false sense of safety. She jumped when he began to speak again.

'As you are so very new to all this, I'll explain what happens now.' His voice was cool and emotionless, yet he continued to stroke her hair, her cheek and the side of her arm as he spoke to her.

'You've disobeyed me twice now in as many days. Hardly a good start, is it?'

'No,' she whispered when she realised that he required a reply. She felt like a recalcitrant schoolgirl hauled before the headmaster.

'It's not as if you don't know any better – in spite of your inexperience, you're a natural. But perhaps we should make sure. *You* tell *me* what it was you did wrong.'

Ariane stared at him, not quite believing her ears. He wanted her to recount a list of her so-called 'sins'? Was it a joke? She almost grinned, but, on seeing the thunderous look in his eyes, she dropped her gaze and twisted her lips into a penitent grimace.

'I . . . I came before you'd given your permission?' she said tentatively.

'What makes you think that permission would have been forthcoming?' he asked, raising an eyebrow at her. 'Pleasures have to be earned, not taken. So – you came without permission. And then?'

He'd stopped calling her 'Angel', Ariane realised with an unpleasant jolt. Somehow, that seemed worse than any ranting and raving could have been. Whereas once she had resented his nickname for her, now she knew she would give anything to hear it on his lips again.

'Well?' he prompted her impatiently.

'I . . . I wore a bra this evening . . .'

'When it had been expressly forbidden. The details are important – you will learn to heed them.'

He walked slowly round her, his hands linked loosely behind him, as if considering a particularly taxing problem. Ariane felt a trembling begin, starting in her solar plexus and travelling through her womb to the soft flesh between her legs. The thong-backed briefs she was wearing rubbed against the plump lips of her sex and she shifted her feet slightly, feeling uncomfortable.

'Do you think this is a game?' he asked her suddenly.

Ariane opened her mouth to tell him that she knew very well that it was, but closed it again when she caught sight of his expression. If she gave the wrong answer, it would be over. Finished.

'No,' she whispered, 'no, I don't think that it's a game.'

'Good. Then you understand that transgressions have to be punished, don't you?' His voice was almost kindly and he leaned towards her so that his face was only inches from hers as he waited for her to reply.

Ariane felt almost faint with longing as the kiss of his breath fanned her cheek. Her entire body was taut as a bow. At once she knew that it was the way in which he was dominating her that affected her so. She responded to the sadistic streak in him on a level far deeper than her conscious mind, so that even as, intellectually, she rebelled, on a more primitive plane she was putty in his hands.

'Yes,' she said, her voice small and thready. 'Please, Conrad – please punish me . . .'

# Three

The silence stretched between them for so long that Ariane thought, for a moment, that, having finally manoeuvred her into begging him to punish her, Conrad would refuse. She knew from past experience that it would be in character, just as she knew that to deny her now would be a harsher punishment than she could bear.

Opening her eyes, she gave him an anguished glance. He smiled at her, the first sign of affection he had displayed since she had arrived, and Ariane was reassured.

'Since you asked so nicely,' he said, laying to rest her fear that he would leave her wanting, 'how can I refuse? What would you like? The crop? A cane? Or a simple spanking?'

Ariane's eyes had widened to saucers as he spoke. The conversation had taken on an almost surreal quality to her and she wasn't sure how she should reply.

'I . . . I've never done anything like this before,' she admitted nervously.

Conrad regarded her thoughtfully.

'Very well. In future you will select your own instrument of chastisement. It adds to the anticipation, I find. Tonight, I will guide you.'

'Thank you,' Ariane whispered, feeling foolish.

She knew that now was the time to leave if she was having second thoughts. He wouldn't stop her, indeed, he appeared to be waiting once more for her to make a decision, as if making sure of her every step of the way. Ariane had no intention of leaving. The excitement churning through her was too powerful to resist, her curiosity propelling her through to the bedroom as he opened the door and stood back to let her pass.

It was a typical, anonymous hotel room, though comfortable enough. There was a bed, covered in a sky blue satin bedspread which matched the ruched blind, drawn across the window. The dressing table and wardrobe were of limed oak, giving the room a light, airy feel that darker furniture would have suppressed.

Ariane watched as Conrad rearranged the pillows, one at the head of the bed, two halfway down it. She began to tremble again as she realised that he wanted her to lie across them, so that the single pillow was beneath her head with the other two supporting her stomach.

On shaking legs, she climbed onto the bed and lay face down. As the pillows forced her bottom up, she felt the short skirt bunch up around her waist, exposing her buttocks, neatly dissected by the thong of her panties. Closing her eyes against the shame of displaying herself thus, Ariane pressed her cheek into the coolness of the pillow and held her breath, letting it out on a sigh when nothing happened.

Conrad spent a long time simply looking at her. Silently, he rearranged her skirt to his liking, pressed her knees further apart and caressed her ankles, his fingertips running along to the dangerous tips of her stiletto-heeled mules.

'That's good,' he said at last. 'Push your bottom up higher . . . that's it. The cane, I think. Harsh enough to hurt, but not to damage. You have such beautiful skin – perfect for marking.'

Ariane sucked in her breath, as much at his words as at the all-too-brief touch of his hand as he traced her curves. She lay very still, listening to him opening a suitcase, but not daring to look round in case he reverted to the cold, frightening mood he had displayed on her arrival.

He laid a thin, whippy looking cane by her cheek, where she could see it. Bending low, he placed his lips against the back of her ear and murmured, 'Don't move. Stay exactly as you are.'

To her surprise, he straightened and walked out of the room, leaving her alone.

Ariane waited, five minutes, ten minutes. By fifteen minutes her back was aching, her arms and legs were beginning to cramp and she was feeling rather foolish. Was he going to come back at all? She could hear the low murmur of the television set in the adjoining room and pictured him, sprawled on the sofa, watching TV. Had he forgotten about her entirely?

Only the thought of his displeasure if she disobeyed him a third time kept her still. This must be one of his tests, to see if she was worthy of the game.

The cane loomed large by her cheek, its smooth surface deceptively innocent looking. Though she had no experience, Ariane guessed that the instrument he had chosen would be whippy enough to sting. Though she trembled at the thought of him caning her, she knew she wanted nothing more than for him to come back, to get on with it.

His pleasure when he returned five minutes later and saw that she hadn't moved out of position made the cramping of her limbs worthwhile. She basked in the glow of his approval, welcoming the warm caress of his palm as he stroked her exposed buttocks, sensitising the skin.

'Such dedication almost cancels out your other transgressions,' he told her, chuckling softly as she was unable to stifle a soft mewl of instinctive protest. 'But that would hardly be fair on you, now would it? No doubt you've been looking forward to the kiss of the cane – isn't that right, Angel?'

She was his Angel again. Possessed of a strange joy, Ariane turned her face towards him and smiled.

'Help me?' she asked him. 'Tell me what to do.'

Conrad smiled almost tenderly at her.

'You don't have to *do* anything,' he assured her, 'except weep a little, perhaps. I will consider your tears a tribute, a measure of your gratitude.'

Ariane braced herself as he stroked the velvety skin of her buttocks one more time before picking up the cane and flexing it. She heard it whistle as it cut through the air, then it landed, with an excruciating *thwack* across the fleshiest part of her buttocks. She screamed, unable to help herself.

'Enough! If you scream again, I will have to gag you. Do you understand?'

'Yes,' she whimpered, her attention focused on the stripe of pain dissecting her buttocks.

Conrad raised his arm again, aiming slightly below the first stripe.

'Aah!'

Ariane cried out again, tears springing to her eyes. She hadn't dreamed it could be so *painful*. Sensing Conrad's irritation, she attempted an apology, but, to her shame, only managed a hiccoughing sob.

'Don't worry,' he consoled her as he tied a black silk scarf tightly around her mouth, 'soon you will feel the pleasure.'

Seriously doubting him now, Ariane endured another blow, swiftly followed by two more. Each time, she realised, Conrad was careful to place the cane in a different spot, so that at the end of the five strokes, her bottom felt as though it was on fire. She was sobbing freely, her tears running down her face and soaking into the gag so that she could taste the salty wetness.

Strange things were beginning to happen within her body. Gradually, she realised that beneath the pain there was another, more powerful sensation spreading through her.

'Again?' Conrad said, and Ariane found herself nodding, welcoming the fiery swipe of the cane twice more.

Conrad came round to the head of the bed and lifted her chin in the crook of his forefinger. His eyes shone as he saw the tears glittering on her lashes and he wiped them away from her cheeks gently with the pad of his thumb.

'Beautiful,' he whispered.

Reaching round her head, he untied the gag and leaned forward to kiss her on the mouth. Ariane closed her eyes, conscious of the pressure building between her thighs, an insistent throbbing in her sex as well as in her poor, abused behind.

Conrad licked away her tears, his tongue passing lightly across the fragile skin of her eyelids and probing the corners of her mouth.

'My Angel . . . sweet slave . . .'

Ariane gasped as he suddenly, unexpectedly, brought his bare hand down on her burning buttocks. He spanked her three, four times, the crack of flesh on flesh shockingly loud in the quiet of the small room. As he did it, he watched her face, seeing at once when her expression changed from endurance to ecstasy.

'Yes, Angel – come.'

It was all she needed. Pressing her hips into the cushions she allowed the rolling waves of orgasm to break over her. He hadn't so much as touched her sex, and yet she climaxed at his command, panting as it went on and on, leaving her exhausted.

Opening her eyes, she saw that Conrad was watching her intently, as if absorbing every nuance of her expression. She was overcome by a rush of pure love for him and she smiled.

'Thank you,' she said, her voice breaking on a sob of emotion. She knew, without a doubt, that once would never be enough. To be his Angel she would endure any humiliation, would cry rivers full of tears, if that was what pleased him. And she knew, with a clarity that astounded her that, whether she wanted it or not, Conrad had seen something in her, a need that he could fulfil. She was lost.

Jon watched Melissa as she flicked a stray strand of her long, dark hair out of her face before starting on the rich chocolate mousse placed before them. She was so different to Ariane, the one so dark with a pale, slender, elegant beauty, the other blonde with a typical English Rose complexion and a pretty, curvaceous figure. And yet there was something . . . something he couldn't quite put his finger on, that was similar about them.

His eyes dropped to Melissa's mouth. Her lips were full, painted a deep, berry red. At the moment they were sucking the thick, rich chocolate off the silver spoon. Jon felt warm as he imagined the cool mousse slipping down her throat. There was something so sensual about the way she was eating that affected him far too strongly for comfort.

He watched now as her pink tongue licked every last drop of the mousse from her spoon, as unselfconsciously as a child licks out a cake bowl, and he shivered.

Melissa looked up at that moment and he recognised the sparkle in her eyes. She knew the effect she was having on him, the shameless minx. Jon felt a surge of emotion, deep and dark and uncomfortable, and he looked away quickly, afraid that her all-seeing eyes would detect it.

'What did you think of the film?' he asked her, aware that, though they had been in the restaurant now for over two hours, they hadn't exchanged the usual views and opinions. They hadn't, in fact, resorted to small talk at all and he felt a sudden, urgent need for mundanity.

Melissa's luscious lips curved into a small, mocking smile.

'It was passably good. Do you go to the cinema often with Ariane?'

Jon frowned. Melissa showed a curiosity about Ariane that he found inexplicable.

'Sometimes. What about you and Luke?' he countered.

Melissa laughed softly.

'Touché.'

She gazed at him consideringly, her head slightly on one side. 'It makes you awkward, talking about our partners, doesn't it?'

Jon felt uncomfortable.

'I suppose it does, a little.'

'Why?'

Picking up his wine glass, Jon stalled for time while he took a sip.

'I don't know,' he admitted finally, returning her intense gaze without flinching.

'Don't you?' she said softly.

She was leaning forward in her seat and her dark hair fell across her cheeks. Jon had to suppress the urge to reach out and brush it back tenderly. Where the inclination had come from, he didn't know, but he was aware that it was becoming stronger, more compelling, by the minute.

'What do you mean?' he asked her.

The words emerged as a hoarse whisper, but Melissa merely

gave him another small, enigmatic smile, and signalled to the waiter that they were ready for the bill.

In the taxi on the way home, Jon watched Melissa covertly. She appeared to be looking out of the window, but he sensed that she was aware of his scrutiny. Her long legs were crossed, one over the other, and the skirt of her dress had ridden up to mid-thigh. As he watched, she uncrossed her legs, recrossing them on the other side, and he caught a brief, tantalising glimpse of suspender.

Jon had an instant erection. All evening he had been aware of her. In the cinema he had breathed in her subtle perfume – a woody, flowery scent overlying the richer, more exciting feminine odours. They had been sitting so closely together that he could feel the heat of her, was conscious of the beat of her heart. Never had he found watching a woman eat a more sensual experience and now he longed to touch her, to *possess* her.

She turned her head at the very moment when the thought ran through his mind. Jon could tell from the look on her face that she had guessed what he was thinking, and he steeled himself for rejection. To his surprise, she merely smiled at him, before turning away to resume looking out of the window.

'Are you coming up?' she asked when they pulled up outside her apartment.

Jon hesitated, torn between desire and loyalty to Ariane. Melissa touched him lightly on the knee and laughed softly.

'Your honour is quite safe with me, Jon. We could have coffee.'

He grinned.

'Am I that transparent? Okay – coffee would be great.'

Melissa's apartment shocked him. Painted in stark white, there were no internal walls whatsoever. Designated living areas were divided variously by *objets d'art*; huge, green plants; a bookshelf, sculpturally shaped, the books arranged more for aesthetic effect than for content. Even the bathroom was part of the whole, the lavatory visible through the thin paper screen pulled across it.

One wall was made entirely of glass from three feet off the ground. Below them, Manhattan spread like a giant, neon-spangled carpet, the sounds and smells of the street below masked by the insulated glass.

Melissa walked around the vast room, switching on strategically placed lamps until the entire space was filled with light and shadow. It was then that Jon realised that there were no blinds, no drapes, nothing to cover the window which ran the length and height of the apartment.

'Well?' she asked him, slipping off her evening jacket. 'What do you think?'

'It's stunning,' he replied at once, 'but so exposed!'

A curious expression passed fleetingly across Melissa's face.

'That was Conrad's idea. He . . .' she glanced away and shrugged slightly. 'What would you like to drink?' she asked him, deciding, it seemed, not to elaborate further.

'Why do you always refer to your lover by his last name? It seems . . . so cold.'

Melissa shrugged and, turning away, she opened a large drinks cabinet.

'It suits us,' she said. 'How about bourbon?'

'I thought you were offering coffee.'

'I feel the need for something more. Won't you join me?'

Her eyes held a challenge and Jon rose to it at once.

'On the rocks?' he asked.

'How else?' She smiled.

He watched her walk towards him, aware of the contours of her body beneath the fluid fabric of her dress. The air was thick with tension, heavy with sensual promise.

'What shall we drink to?' she asked, passing him a glass and touching it with her own.

Jon looked down into her lambent brown eyes and suddenly found it painful to breathe. She was gazing up at him as if she adored him, as if he was the only man in the world for her at that moment. It made him feel . . . strong, a man in the traditional, hunter-gatherer mould with pride of ownership in his woman. Only Melissa wasn't his woman, he reminded himself abruptly.

'To international relations?' he managed, shakily.

Melissa's smile was ironic.

'To friendship,' she amended, her voice a low, seductive purr.

She swayed slightly towards him as she lifted the glass to her lips and swallowed. Jon's eyes were transfixed by her mouth and the rippling of her throat and he knew, without a doubt, that he didn't want to go home to his lonely hotel room tonight.

Slowly, he lowered his head so that he could feel her soft breath brush against his lips. She didn't move away, though she waited passively for him to kiss her. They both jumped violently as the telephone rang, its shrill note discordant, shattering the mood of intimacy that had enfolded them.

'I'm sorry,' Melissa said, grimacing slightly. 'Please – relax, make yourself at home. Have a seat here and enjoy your drink – I'll be back!'

Jon watched her as she picked up the portable telephone and carried it to the bed at the far corner of the apartment. He heard her answer, then her voice dropped to a low murmur as the caller identified him or herself.

Glancing around him, Jon saw that there was a huge, cream leather sofa facing towards the window-wall. Putting his drink on the glass-topped coffee table in front of it, he sat down and gazed out at the night time panorama. It made him feel small, uncomfortably insignificant as he imagined the ebb and flow of city life taking place below him.

When Melissa did not immediately cut her call short and come back, Jon began to feel restless. There was a large, black folder lying on the coffee table, similar to the kind of portfolio art students carried. Idly, Jon picked up the folder, conscious of a waft of fine leather as he moved it. He brought it to his nose and breathed the scent in deeply. There was something satisfyingly sensual about running his fingers over the soft, supple hide, and he realised that this was no student's folder, but a special item to Melissa, something to be treasured.

Slowly, he opened it. His eyebrows rose as he saw a black and white photographic portrait of Melissa in the first transparent sleeve. The medium chosen had exactly caught the air of sensual vulnerability that he found so attractive about her. From the way she was staring into the camera, Jon guessed that the photographer was Luke Conrad. Her eyes looked huge, the expression in them a curious mixture of seduction and innocence.

Jon felt his penis harden and swell as he stared at her eyes, his gaze travelling down to her moist, slightly parted lips. A sudden, shocking image pushed itself into his mind's eye, of those soft, generous lips stretching wide over the head of his cock, drawing it into the heated sanctuary of her mouth . . .

Swallowing hard, Jon flicked over to the next sleeve. In this photograph, she was naked, sitting with her knees drawn up to her chest, her arms hugging them loosely. It was a side view, so there was nothing to be seen of her breasts or sex, and her head and face were covered by a huge picture hat, worn at a slight angle so that it tilted forward. Her long hair had been piled up inside the hat so as not to obscure the sweep of her softly lit, naked limbs.

It was a beautiful photograph, perfectly capturing the velvety texture of her skin and the delicate curve of her long neck. A wisp of dark hair was visible at the nape, an abberation which gave her an air of sweet vulnerability.

Jon was aware that he felt hot. Taking a slug of his drink, he took off his jacket and laid it over the back of the sofa. His hands trembled as he picked up the folder and, making himself comfortable, he turned to the next page.

The image confronting him made him gasp. It was another head and shoulders shot, but this time the whiteness of her face was dissected by a stark streak of black across her mouth. A fleeting sense of outrage at the fact that she had been gagged was swiftly obliterated by another, more primitive emotion that Jon was unwilling to face.

His gaze was drawn to her eyes and the expression of pleading in them. They glistened with tears and her forehead was puckered slightly into a frown – of distress? Jon wasn't sure. The picture was too stylised for him to be certain whether it was a pose, or genuine. All he really knew was that the photograph – or, more accurately, his response to it – both appalled and fascinated him.

There was one more photograph in the book. Jon stared at it for several seconds before he was able to take in the details. Melissa was kneeling this time, facing the camera, with a large mirror behind her so that she could be seen from both front and back. She was naked, except for a strange, harness-like contraption. It consisted of a series of leather straps fastened by large, shiny buckles. The first formed a collar round her neck, the second bound her upper arms, just above her breasts. Each strap was attached to the last by a vertical strip of leather, dissected by the buckles.

Her arms were drawn back behind her and cuffed at the wrists. A third strap was wrapped around her waist, drawn tight so that her breasts were squeezed through the gaps, divided by the two straps above and below and the vertical strip, and pushed out. Her small, dark nipples were prominent, and shiny, as if recently sucked. The idea of that made Jon's mouth run dry.

The thin strap which ran from her throat down the front of her body, passed underneath her and was fastened to the waist strap at the small of her back by a large metal loop. It had been pulled tight, so that it fitted snugly into her sex. Her mons was shaved, so her labia were clearly visible on either side of the strap, swollen and puffy, as if she had been wearing the restraint for a long time.

Dragging his eyes away from the sight of her shaven quim, Jon gazed at her face. Her mouth was open, as if waiting to receive something inside it, her head tilted back so that her eyes appeared half closed. She looked wanton, submissive, yet totally abandoned, and he felt his cock twitch inside his trousers.

'Do you like my photographs?'

He'd been so engrossed, he hadn't noticed that Melissa had finished her phone call. Jumping guiltily as he heard her voice, he closed the portfolio abruptly and laid it on the coffee table.

Melissa was standing a few feet away, watching him in that curiously intent way she had, as if trying to read him. There was a tension about her, a rigidity in the way she held herself, that hadn't been there before.

'They're very beautiful,' Jon replied honestly.

She smiled, clearly pleased by his response. Moving towards him, she knelt at his feet. Jon held his breath, hardly daring to hope that he had correctly interpreted the look on her face. She

51

gazed up at him, through her lashes, a wealth of promise in her dark eyes.

When she placed her palm gently over the bulge in his trousers, he let out his breath on a ragged sigh.

'May I?' she asked softly.

Jon was unable to do anything but nod. He could hardly believe this was happening – a beautiful woman was kneeling at his feet, deftly unfastening his trousers. As she cupped his burning shaft in her palm, Jon closed his eyes for a moment, relishing the sensation of her soft, cool skin against the heat of his.

Her fingertips played across his scrotum, caressing the skin which was stretched tightly across his balls. He felt full to bursting, the slow seduction she had played all evening finally coming to a crisis point.

Expertly, Melissa eased his foreskin back to reveal the peach-soft tip, running her thumbnail gently along the tiny slit. Watching her, Jon saw his cock begin to weep with the clear fluid of pre-emission as she ran her hand back and forth, moving the skin over the hard core of his penis.

It took control to stop himself from coming there and then, but he was curious to see how far she would go. He could see her nipples pressing against the clingy fabric of her dress and was pleased to see evidence that she was aroused by her own actions.

When she dipped her head and stretched her lips wide across the head of his cock, Jon felt as if he had died and gone to heaven. It was everything he had hoped for, and more, for no fantasy could ever compare with the reality of her soft, hot mouth enclosing him, drawing him in.

He felt her tongue probe the slippery crease before she sucked gently, drawing the salty fluid from him. Her cheeks bulged as she took more of him inside her mouth, and her soft hair caressed his inner thighs, sending little ripples of pleasure through to his belly.

Over her head, he could see the lights of the city, and no longer felt small and insignificant. Now he felt as though he was king of it all. Surveying his realm with a gorgeous concubine sucking his cock, Jon felt powerful, ten feet tall.

Reaching down, he ran his fingers through her hair, fanning it out and letting it fall in a silky shawl around her shoulders. Overcome by a desire to see her naked skin, he reached down and unbuttoned the top two buttons of her dress so that he could ease it down, off her shoulders.

Her skin was pale, milky-white, almost translucent in the subdued lighting. As if the images were indelibly tattooed behind his eyelids, Jon saw again the pleading, sultry expression in her eyes as they glittered with tears. Knowing that her quim was completely hairless gave him a deeply resonating thrill, and he imagined fastening the leather strap so that it divided the sweet, slippery lips of her sex, knowing that it would rub against the sensitised flesh, keeping her in a state of perpetual readiness . . .

He was coming, the seed pumping along his shaft and bursting, in a series of long, blissful spurts, into Melissa's willing mouth. She swallowed hard, sucking at him until there was nothing left and his cock began to soften in her mouth.

Only then did she pull back, running her tongue around her lips in a gesture so erotic that Jon felt a glimmer of response from his sated cock. She smiled at him, and, sitting back on her heels, pressed her hand against her mons. Holding his eye, she rubbed her palm back and forth, stimulating herself through the thin fabric of her dress until, with a shudder, she curled her fingers against her sex and pressed hard against her clitoris.

'Oh-h!' she sighed, rocking back on her heels and closing her eyes.

Jon sank down onto the floor in front of her and cupped her face in his hands. Melissa opened her eyes and he saw the dying light of ecstasy in them. Overcome with some nameless, wonderful emotion, he kissed her eyes, her cheeks, the corners of her mouth and her chin. She was trembling, still quivering with the effects of her climax, and he gave in to the urge to gather her in his arms and hold her while the convulsions subsided.

After a few minutes, she disentangled herself gently and stood up.

'Please go now,' she said softly.

Jon's first reaction was to protest, to tell her that he wanted to stay and love her properly, but the words died on his lips as he saw her expression. It was a mixture of uncertainty, and lingering excitement, and he knew instinctively that the longer they preserved the freshness of their relationship, the more satisfying it would be for both of them.

'All right,' he said, surprised to hear how calm his voice sounded.

He did not try to touch her again, he merely rearranged his clothing and pushed his arms into his jacket. Some sixth sense told him that it was for him to take the initiative now.

'Tomorrow night,' he told her, as if by fellating him she had already given her consent to whatever else he might require. 'In my hotel room this time.'

She didn't answer, but Jon did not doubt that she would be there. Something told him that, as far as Melissa was concerned, his instincts would stand him in good stead.

As he left her and stepped out into the cool night, he felt as though he was walking on air.

# *Four*

Ariane listened as Conrad spoke to Melissa on the telephone. She had no choice but to listen: he had tied her to the overhead shower attachment in the bathroom and was sitting on the bathroom stool with his mobile telephone.

Trying to ignore the burning ache in her upstretched arms, Ariane listened to his side of the conversation jealously. He used the same tone to Melissa that he used when he spoke to her, but he called the other girl 'baby' and 'honey' not 'Angel', and for that, Ariane was grateful.

'Are you alone, baby?' he asked when she answered.

'No? Who are you with?'

Conrad chuckled as he was told, and glanced at Ariane. All her senses prickled with awareness.

'Is he hot for you? Yes? Are you turned on? Okay. I wish I was there too, honey . . .' he winked at Ariane when he said this, as if to reassure her that he didn't really want to be anywhere else but here with her.

She hadn't gone home after the caning the night before. Afterwards, Conrad had been so tender towards her, bathing her and washing her hair, then drying it with the hotel hairdryer. He had played the cool air over her burning buttocks and made sure she was comfortable on her stomach before she slept.

He didn't sleep in the same bed. Ariane had felt so exhausted that she hadn't gone to investigate, assuming that he had chosen to sleep on the couch in the living room.

In the morning, room service brought them warm, crumbly croissants which Conrad spread with thick, creamy butter and strawberry jam. Breaking them into bite-sized pieces, he had fed them to her, bit by bit, holding a glass of orange juice to her lips for her to sip from.

It wasn't until lunchtime that he had asked if she would allow him to tie her in the bathroom. *Asked* her. Ariane had been so taken aback, she had agreed at once. Now she was wondering if she had done the right thing. So far, all he had done was strip and bind her, before telephoning his girlfriend in America!

'Don't let him touch you, honey,' he was saying now, 'not tonight . . . you can frig yourself in front of him . . . yes, that would be good. Here's what you're to do. Walk over to him and kneel in front of him. Ask his permission to touch him . . . yes . . . of course you can, baby . . . do it for me . . .'

His voice had taken on the crooning, coaxing tone that habitually turned Ariane's legs to water. She wondered if the faceless girl at the other end of the telephone was feeling the same way. Was she lying on her bed, quivering with desire? Did she long for him to tell her to touch herself, to give her permission to come?

'I want you to suck him, baby. And swallow, every last drop.' He laughed softly and Ariane saw that his eyes glowed with pleasure. 'I know you don't like it, baby. That's why I want you to do it. I'll phone you tomorrow and you can tell me all about it . . . Sure, I'm okay.'

Glancing across at Ariane, he smiled at her.

'I'm kind of busy right now, honey . . . that's right. She's very pretty, very . . . amenable. Go and suck that cock now, honey.'

He broke the connection and, putting the phone aside, gave Ariane a wolfish smile.

'Now,' he said, standing up and coming towards her, 'where were we?'

It took Jon a long time to get to sleep once he left Melissa. Curiously, although it was the first time he had ever been unfaithful to Ariane, he couldn't seem to work up what he considered to be sufficient regret, or guilt. True, he hadn't actually screwed Melissa, but the encounter between them had been intimate enough for it to be considered a betrayal. The fact that there was an ocean the size of the Atlantic between them was no excuse, and yet he had the strangest feeling that what he was doing with Melissa didn't count.

It bothered him, this apparent lack of concern for Ariane. Normally, he made her the centre of his world and would never do anything to jeopardise her happiness. But the feelings he had experienced while he was with Melissa had been so strong, so new, he felt compelled to explore them. Certainly, he knew that now those feelings had been awakened, if he didn't find out more he would always remember, and wonder what it was he had missed.

When, at last, he fell asleep, his rest was fractured by a series of disjointed, intensely erotic dreams which chased each other relentlessly through his mind. In his dreamscape, Ariane and Melissa merged into one, their faces superimposing themselves one on the other, their arms and legs merging to create one, eponymous whole.

The mouth that smiled at him was Ariane's mouth, yet as he slipped his burgeoning cock inside it, it felt like Melissa's. It was Ariane who looked adoringly up at him, but with Melissa's expression.

Tossing and turning restlessly, Jon pictured himself making love to both women in every position he knew, and some he didn't know he knew, their bodies and faces shifting in and out of focus, shockingly interchangeable.

He pictured himself strapping them both into the leather harness he had seen in the photograph, the thrill he had experienced at the sight surging up through his subconscious, translating itself into an erection. Waking with it still aching the next morning, Jon brought himself to a lonely climax in the shower, wondering where it would all lead.

Acknowledging that he wanted them both was one thing, but he was aware that there was one important element in the whole affair, the reactions of whom he had deliberately refused to address. Luke Conrad.

Conrad lathered the soap between his palms and began to massage it into Ariane's skin. It smelled of roses and tickled her nose as he massaged her neck, then focused on the stretched sinews of her armpits and arms.

Though there was some discomfort caused by being bound in such a position for so long, Ariane was relieved to discover that 'the game', as she had come to privately think of her relationship with Conrad, did not always involve tears. His touch now was firm, but gentle and he seemed solicitous of her pleasure.

His hands were warm and slippery, sliding across the damp surface of her skin as he washed her. Lingering on the soft areolae which crowned her breasts, he stroked and caressed them until they had risen into two aching peaks of need.

Moving lower, he circled the gentle swell of her belly, causing a referred pressure to build between her thighs, She moaned, softly. Smiling, Conrad moved forward to kiss her, capturing the small sound in his own mouth. His fingers were warm as they curled into the soft, secret flesh of her sex and Ariane felt a fresh rush of moisture seep between the folds.

He soaped her there, and between her buttocks, his fingertips circling the small, puckered rose of her anus until she clenched her buttocks reflexively, earning herself a raised eyebrow more eloquent than any words. Slowly, she forced her bottom cheeks to relax and he stroked the sensitive skin around her forbidden orifice until she trembled with renewed apprehension.

When he moved his hand away, she shivered with a mixture of relief and disappointment. Conrad regarded her enigmatically, reaching behind her to detach the shower head from the wall. Ariane gasped as he turned on the shower and a spray of warm water hit her breasts and stomach. The water cascaded over her skin, trickling between her thighs and mixing with the thicker, heavier dew of her arousal. Conrad untied her so that she could turn around and he rinsed her all over, not allowing her to step out of the shower until he was satisfied that all the suds had swirled down the plughole.

Ariane closed her eyes as he wrapped her in the huge, fluffy towel which had been warming on the radiator. Standing absolutely still, she waited for him to dry her. It was like being a doll – it seemed that nothing was required of her except her reactions.

'Why are you doing this?' she asked him as he knelt at her feet and, picking up one, dried between her toes.

'Because it pleases me,' he replied, tapping her other foot lightly to indicate that she should lift it for him.

'I don't understand. Last night you were so . . . cold, and yet since then you have been so gentle . . .'

Conrad stood eye to eye to her for the first time. His expression was inscrutable and Ariane felt the dark tug of desire in her stomach which was becoming all too familiar whenever he looked at her.

'There are two sides to every coin,' he answered her cryptically. 'I enjoy bathing you, caring for you. I adore you.'

'You do?' she asked faintly. The verb sounded a trifle extreme. Conrad smiled slightly, as if he was aware of her thoughts and was amused by them.

'Of course. Haven't you ever been cherished before?'

*Cherished.* It was a lovely word, a word that warmed her, addressing, as it did, her deepest desires.

'No,' she admitted after a moment. 'I've been loved, but never cherished.'

Conrad stepped away from her and picked up a dry towel. 'Then trust me, Angel, I will show you a world you only ever dreamed existed.'

Ariane followed him, and knew that she would wherever he asked her to go. And Jon? She pushed the thought of him away, unwilling to think about the implications this would have on her relationship with her fiancé. All she really knew was that Conrad had shown her what was missing, that elusive ingredient to her sex life for which she had searched fruitlessly for so long. How could she have found it when she had no idea what she was looking for?

'Lie down on the bed.'

Conrad's voice interrupted her thoughts and she started slightly. He had spread the fresh towel on the bed. On the table beside it, there was a tray with a razor, a pot of shaving cream and scissors, set out like a surgeon's tools.

'Wh-what are you doing?' she asked, alarm making her voice rise.

'Lie down, on your back, please,' he asked her again with exaggerated patience.

'But—'

'Don't you trust me?'

There was an edge of steel in his voice that made her obey him, though her arms and legs were shaking as she climbed onto the bed and lay, on her back, on the towel. Her legs were clamped tightly together, and Conrad ran his forefinger lightly down the crease between them, his eyes mocking her gently.

'Such modesty!' he said, his voice low and silky.

Ariane began to tremble in quite a different way as he pushed her legs apart and bent them up at the knees.

'Oh!' she cried, embarrassed by the way he was exposing her so ruthlessly.

Ignoring the small sound of distress, Conrad eased a pillow beneath her hips, so that her pelvis was tipped up and her sex was open and vulnerable. Stepping back, he looked at her, his expression unreadable.

'Please . . .' Ariane whispered, mortified by his scrutiny.

'Please?'

'I . . . I can't bear it . . . please, Conrad – it embarrasses me!'

Suddenly, his face changed. His eyebrows drew together sharply and his lips thinned as he walked to the head of the bed and put his face close to hers. Ariane's eyes widened fearfully and she flinched away from the anger emanating from his every pore.

'It *embarrasses* you? What difference do you think that makes? If you can't set your sense of self aside, you will never learn, never understand!'

He spoke so passionately, and by the time he had finished, his anger seemed to have dissipated. Risking its return, she asked him in a small voice,

'Why do you like to hurt and humiliate me?'

Conrad looked surprised by the question as he straightened. Then he smiled, a small upward curve of his lips which was without warmth.

'Because it's what you need.'

Not what she *liked*, or what she *wanted*, but what she needed.

'You're wrong,' she whispered, her voice lacking conviction even to her own ears.

'Tell me that the next time you beg me to punish you, my Angel. Walk away *then*, and I'll believe you.'

He watched the play of emotions across her features as she struggled with what he had said. To accept that there was something in her that *needed* to be sexually dominated, that revelled in her submission, was a travesty of everything she had ever imagined she knew about herself. Even now, though, she had lain as he had arranged her, making no attempt to close her legs, her arousal undiminished even in the face of his sudden anger.

Conrad read the reluctant agreement in her eyes and smiled at her.

'I want to shave you – nothing else.'

'Why?' she asked, her voice small.

He sighed, and Ariane realised she had disappointed him again.

'Isn't it enough that I want it? Do you have to have an explanation for everything?'

Ariane shook her head.

'I'm sorry.'

'Then we can start?'

'Yes.'

She watched him as he carried the tray to the far end of the bed and pulled up a chair so that he could sit between her legs. With his eyes on her open sex, Ariane imagined she could feel the moisture seeping slowly from her and her face burned with shame. She sucked in her breath as he placed his hand on her mound, ruffling the soft mat of her pubic hair.

'You'll like it when it's done,' he promised her as he picked up the scissors.

Unconvinced, Ariane lay passively as he trimmed the hair down to the skin and wiped it away with a warm flannel. Her heart was beating erratically in her chest and she hardly dared to breathe as he worked in the shaving cream and picked up the razor. Supposing he cut her? Realising in that moment just how much trust she was placing in him, Ariane swallowed, hard, and closed her eyes.

'Open your eyes,' he said at once. 'I want you to watch.'

There was no question in her mind that she wouldn't obey him. The head of the razor felt ominously cold as it touched against her exposed flesh. Starting just below her belly, he shaved her with short, careful strokes, denuding her of the covering of hair until the beginning of her crease was fully exposed.

Ariane was aware of a pulse beating steadily in the nub of her clitoris and she marvelled that such a hazardous experience could arouse her. But it *was* arousing her, there was no hiding the fact. The heavy dew of desire trickled along her perineum and between her buttocks, seeping into the towel beneath her.

Seeing it, Conrad scooped some up in his fingers and, to her horror, pressed them against her lips.

'Suck,' he said when she did not immediately open her mouth.

Reluctantly, she obeyed him, tasting the sea-spray saltiness of

63

her own secretions as she licked his fingers clean. He watched her mouth, his eyes avid, the pupils dilated so that there was no more than a thin topaz ring around them.

'You see how good trust can taste?' he murmured.

Turning his attention back to the task in hand, he prolonged the anticipation by going into the bathroom to fetch fresh water. Ariane knew that her labia were swollen and moist, protruding below the outer lips which he would want to depilate. Despite her nervousness, however, she knew that she did indeed trust him, and she marvelled at how he had managed to gain her trust in such a short period of time.

Her breathing was shallow as he repositioned himself between her knees and picked up the razor. With his other hand, he massaged more cream into the outer lips, his fingers brushing against the more sensitive inner labia, increasing her arousal.

He opened her with two fingers either side, peeling the folds of skin apart, then he slid one finger along one slippery channel and stroked the head of the razor along the skin. Ariane hardly dared to breathe now. She focused all her attention on Conrad's dark head, inches away from her sex.

His expression was intent, his concentration absolute as he repeated the procedure on the other side. Finally, he shaved the area on either side of her perineum, his fingertips pressing lightly against her anal sphincter as he held her open.

Ariane breathed a sigh of relief as Conrad went to fetch a warm flannel. Her sex felt odd as he blotted it meticulously with the flannel. She hardly dared to look.

'Have you finished?' she asked him.

'Almost. Be patient – I'll bring you a mirror in a moment.'

First, he massaged a generous amount of moisturising cream into the exposed skin, his fingers dabbling freely in the thick, honeyed juices which flowed freely from her.

'My little wanton,' he teased her, his fingertips fluttering tantalisingly close to the stem of her clitoris.

Ariane swallowed and tried to concentrate on anything but the pleasant sensations rioting through her. Silently, she begged him not to touch that most sensitive of spots directly, for, if he did, she knew that she would come at once, permission or no.

As their eyes met, Ariane realised that Conrad was aware of this. He smiled cruelly at her as his fingers circled the hard little bead and she thought that he would tip her over the edge merely for the pleasure of punishing her afterwards. Though she acknowledged that a part of her was half hoping that this is what he would do, she was aware that her mouth had run dry and she was focusing all her attention on not coming. She was rewarded by his sudden smile.

'Well done, my Angel. How quickly you learn!'

Turning away, he went to fetch the mirror from the bathroom. Positioning it between her legs, he watched her face as she stared at herself.

'Beautiful, isn't it?'

Ariane's eyes widened as she saw the naked mound between her legs. Her sex looked so vulnerable, so available to whatever pleasures he devised and she shivered involuntarily. Bringing her knees down, she saw that her inner labia protruded slightly below the outer, the smooth, shiny flesh shockingly pink against the paler skin outside.

'You have a pretty quim,' he told her, tugging gently at the moist folds. 'If I was here for longer, I would stretch these for you so that they could receive constant stimulation.'

A flush of heat suffused Ariane at the thought, and she wondered whether to be relieved, or disappointed, that there wouldn't be time. It hit her then that he had mentioned leaving, and she felt curiously bereft.

'What will happen when you go?' she asked impulsively, aware that she did not want to think about it.

'Lie back,' he said, ignoring her question, 'I want to taste you.'

'Oh no, I don't like oral sex, I—'

'Are you refusing me?'

His voice was calm and reasonable, but his eyes were turbulent as he looked at her. Ariane recognised the storm clouds gathering behind them and was assailed by a rush of desire so strong that she almost fell back against the pillows.

'No,' she whispered, 'please . . . taste me.'

She expected him to dive in, to feel his tongue push its way into her vagina like a cat at a bowl of cream, but Conrad had other ideas. His breath was warm against the soft skin of her inner thighs and she felt the tiny hairs rise as it played over them, As if possessed of a life of their own, her labia opened, like a flower to the sun and she felt his warm breath on the tender inner petals.

The first touch of his tongue was electrifying. So gently, he ran its tip along the dewy channels on either side of her cleft, lapping delicately at the viscous secretions, his approach delicate and unhurried, as if he was about to enjoy a gourmet meal.

Holding her thighs apart with his hands, he swirled his tongue lightly around the gaping entrance to her body before sweeping it up, over the stretched membranes to where her clitoris pulsed at the apex.

Ariane was finding it hard to breathe. Her entire body felt as taut as a bow, her concentration focused on that small area between her legs where, it seemed, all her nerve endings ended. Careful not to touch the supersensitive bud itself, Conrad dabbed his tongue at its base, sending little darts of intense pleasure through to her womb. She felt it cramp as a fresh rush of moisture trickled from her body.

At once, Conrad dipped his head and sucked at the clear, viscous honey, moving his head from side to side as if enjoying it to the full.

'Oh, please,' Ariane gasped, 'please make me come! I can't bear it!'

She hardly recognised her own voice; it was breathless and raw, vibrating with need. Conrad raised his head and looked at her. She could see her own juices on his lips, smearing his chin and her clitoris began to throb with an ever stronger rhythm.

'Very well,' he said.

Ariane recognised the resonance of desire in his tone and thrilled to the knowledge that she was the cause of it. Perhaps this time he would fuck her. For now, though, all she wanted was him to touch her clitoris with his tongue, to release the explosion of energy she could feel building at its base.

He made her wait a little more, seconds which felt like hours.

'Please! Please, please!' she begged him, almost incoherent with need.

'You may come when I give the signal,' he said calmly as he buried his face in her wet flesh again.

Ariane wanted to ask him what the signal was, but his tongue was playing havoc with her senses, quivering back and forth over the tumescent button of her clitoris. The warmth of pre-orgasm swiftly invaded her legs and swept up her torso. Though they had been paid no attention at all, her breasts were aching, her nipples like two shiny cones, and she covered them with her hands, feeling them press against her palms.

It was no good – if he didn't give the signal soon she would lose control. Just as she was sure that she would disgrace herself, Conrad sucked the pulsing promontory between his lips and bit the end gently.

Ariane cried out, her legs scissoring across his shoulders, pulling him closer. Her hips mashed against his face, smothering him as he sucked the life out of the quivering bud. As she peaked, he entered her with two fingers and pressed upward, towards her pubic bone. Ariane felt that she would faint with pleasure. She could feel her juices running down his fingers and wondered at the copiousness of it. Never had she felt so wet, so open, so utterly, gloriously abandoned.

'Oh please, Conrad!' she cried out at the height of her orgasm, 'please come inside me!'

Raising his head, he shifted up the bed and kissed her, his fingers still buried deep inside her body, strumming the sensitive spot on the walls of her vagina.

She could taste her secretions adhering to his lips and tongue and she drank it in gratefully, all her inhibitions gone.

'Fuck me?' she murmured as he drew away. 'Please, please, Conrad – please fuck me!'

His face was inches from hers and she found it difficult to see his expression. She sensed his rejection, though, before he spoke.

'No,' he said.

'But *why*?'

Ariane didn't understand. As he straightened, her eyes flickered to his crotch and she saw the unmistakable tumescence which told her he was as aroused as she. Catching the direction of her confused gaze, Conrad's lips curved slightly.

'It's too soon,' he told her, his face closing against her.

'Too soon? I don't understand. You want me, I know you do. I want you. It's simple—'

'*Simple*?' he interrupted her.

The word seemed to anger him and Ariane bit her lower lip, watching him warily.

'There is nothing simple about this, Angel, at least, not in the way you mean. You must learn not to make demands. Trust me to know what you need, Angel.'

His voice had dropped to the low, mesmeric murmur that never failed to turn her innards to water. He smiled as he saw the change in her expression. Reaching out, he stroked her hair away from her cheek in a gesture so tender it brought tears to her eyes.

'Trust me,' he said.

Ariane pressed her lips against the centre of his palm to signal her agreement.

# Five

When Jon walked into the office the next morning, Melissa was already sitting in the chair behind his desk. Her expression was sombre as she rose to greet him, her eyes not quite meeting his as she spoke.

'Good morning, Jon.'

His heart sank. Had she decided to tell him that last night had been a mistake?

'Melissa – what a lovely surprise! Are you waiting to see me?'

He gave her a confident smile, hoping that she wouldn't be able tell how nervous he felt. She gave no indication of being aware of his discomfort, though there was clearly something worrying her.

'I wanted to talk to you,' she said, walking round the desk to face him.

Jon eyed the long, smooth expanse of her legs beneath the short skirt of her suit and had to suppress an urge to run his hand along her thigh as she rested her bottom on the edge of his desk.

'Oh?' he feigned indifference as he put his case behind the desk and draped his jacket over the back of the chair.

'Yes. About tonight.'

'Ah.'

What would she do if he pushed her onto her back and hooked those gorgeous, long legs over his shoulders? There was hardly anyone in the office to peer over the hardwood partition into his office space. If they were quick . . .

'I think I ought to explain . . .'

'Explain? Are you having second thoughts?'

Melissa shook her head, her eyes dropping from his, as if she didn't want him to see her expression.

'No. I want to come, it's just that . . . I *can't* . . .'

She looked up at him then, her dark eyes pleading with him, asking for understanding.

'Can't?' he echoed.

She shook her head and dropped her gaze again. Acting on impulse, Jon moved close to her and slipped his hand under the heavy curtain of her hair. Melissa looked up, her expression reminding him of a startled fawn. He could smell her perfume and the underlying sweetness of her skin. Her lower lip trembled slightly as Jon's eyes lingered there and he felt again that curious rush of self-confidence, the expansion of his ego which always seemed to result from contact with Melissa.

'Or *won't*?' he whispered, watching as her eyes widened, their expression uncertain.

'I . . . Oh!'

He swallowed her answer by swooping to cover her lips, his tongue drawing the sweetness from her mouth. Taken by surprise, Melissa clutched at him, her body bending into a graceful arc as he grasped the nape of her neck and pulled her head back.

He could feel the gentle swell of her breasts pressing against his chest. With his free hand, he reached around her back and pressed her to him, revelling in the way her softness melded against the masculine, hard contours of his own body. Working his leg between her thighs, he imagined he could feel the heat of her sex through the layers of fabric, and his cock leapt in his pants, nudging against the soft swell of her belly.

Melissa was responding to him, her nipples gathering into hard little peaks against his chest, her hands massaging his shoulders, long nails digging into the firm flesh. From the way the sexual tension made her body vibrate against his, Jon knew that it wasn't *won't*.

'Why can't you?' he asked, when at last they broke apart. He was still holding her, one hand caressing the slender dip of her back while the other meshed in the hair at the nape of her neck. Melissa stared at him, wide-eyed, her lips still parted, swollen from the onslaught of his kiss.

'I . . . Conrad,' she gasped at last. 'I need permission from Conrad.'

Jon scanned her eyes, his brows drawing together in a frown. What the hell was she talking about? Abruptly, he moved away from her, turning away as she struggled to regain her composure.

'You didn't seem to be thinking of Luke Conrad last night,' he said without looking at her.

He felt unaccountably angry, not wanting to be forced to confront his own perfidy in the face of Melissa's belated guilt pangs. Her answer so surprised him that his head shot up and he stared at her in disbelief.

'Of course I was thinking of him. Did you think I would do what I did if I wasn't?'

Jon felt the colour drain out of his face as the full import of her words sank in.

'Why, you—'

He took a step towards her as incredulity swiftly turned to fury. Melissa's expression stopped him in his tracks. She was looking at him calmly, a twinkle of amusement in her dark brown eyes.

'I'm sorry, Jon – I thought you knew. Isn't this the way with you and Ariane?'

'What do you mean?'

'From the way you speak of her, I thought . . .' She gave a small, helpless gesture with one hand, as if at a loss to explain. 'You seemed so . . . knowing, I thought . . . I'm so sorry. I didn't mean to mislead you.'

'Mislead me? What the hell is going on, Melissa? Last night . . . I don't like being taken for a fool!'

She seemed to be about to say something, but they were interrupted by a knock at the door.

'Come in!' Jon growled, angry at the interruption, but unable to think of a feasible reason for ignoring it.

The post boy thrust the day's mail into his hand without so much as a glance into the room, his appearance merely a pleat in the flow of events. Jon waited until they were alone again before facing Melissa. All his anger seemed to have dissipated now and he looked at her steadily.

'I would like you to come tonight, all the same.'

'Really, I—'

'You owe me an explanation, at least,' he interrupted her.

Melissa shook her head and he felt a swift, uncontrollable pang of desire as her breasts shook beneath the filmy fabric of her blouse.

'I don't owe you anything, Jon,' she said quietly, 'but I will come to talk. Maybe . . .'

'What?'

She shook her head again, her lips curving in a small, self-deprecating smile.

'We'll see. Later.'

Then she was gone and only her perfume lingered in the cool, air-conditioned room.

Ariane fidgeted on the stool at her drawing board. She couldn't concentrate on her work and her mind kept replaying the events of that morning over and over again.

'*Trust me to know what you need*,' he had said.

Did she trust him? Yes, and no. Yes, because he had been right about her every time so far. Never before had she met a man who could interpret her every desire before even she was aware of it. No, because she didn't think he realised how much she wanted him.

It was almost as if she had to earn the privilege of intercourse. She'd never thought of making love in such terms before. To her it had always seemed to be the most natural expression of love, or pure lust, between a man and a woman. Simple, uncomplicated, appealing to both parties. Conrad, by showing no interest whatsoever in fucking her, had turned those beliefs inside out.

Ariane could not understand how he could hold himself back. What had he got out of their relationship so far? She knew that he was aroused by her, that he was perfectly capable of achieving and sustaining an erection, she had seen it often enough to know that he didn't have any problems in that respect. Did he go away to masturbate after he had been with her?

Even as she asked herself these questions, Ariane knew, with some instinct she hadn't known she possessed, that it was Conrad's formidable self-control that was the key. For, not only did he like to control her, and her responses, he also liked to push himself to the limits of endurance, almost as if he prided himself on his ability to restrain his own orgasm.

The more Ariane saw of Conrad, the more she admired him – and the more her desire for him grew. By denying her the one thing she wanted from him, he kept her keen, kept her coming back for more in the hope that *this* time, he would possess her as she yearned to be possessed.

Oh yes, he was very clever. Before he had dressed her and brought her back to the flat late that morning, he had smiled and told her he had a gift for her.

'I can't see you for a few days,' he said, chuckling softly when she was unable to hide her dismay at the prospect. 'I know, Angel, I'll miss you, too. But then again, a little self-discipline will be good for you. Absence makes the heart grow fonder, so they say. I want you to wear this, so you won't forget me.'

As if she could forget him! He had produced a thin leather belt which he fastened around her naked waist, making sure it was tight enough not to slip, without digging in to her soft flesh. There was a small metal ring attached to the buckle with another attached to the point which rested at the small of her back.

Smiling at her bewilderment, Conrad showed her the device which linked the two metal loops. It too was made of leather, though this was a fine, supple hide. Some three inches from either end, the leather was split vertically, forming a narrow slit some six inches long.

'This will remind you of me,' he told her, his fingertips caressing the soft skin of her lower lip. 'Every time you move, you will think of me and what we do together.'

He attached the thin leather strap to the front of the belt, then passed it between her legs, across her newly depilated mound. Ariane had gasped as she experienced the friction caused against her sensitive labia, bending at the knees so that he could reach between her legs and fasten the other end of the strap to the second metal loop.

The strap was pulled tight so that it nestled into the soft, moist folds of her sex. Conrad adjusted it so that her clitoris was pushed into the slit, the two halves of the split settling as if especially tailored for her, into the tender channels between her inner and outer lips.

She had closed her eyes as he stroked her bound sex, making the juices flow, just enough to reawaken her desire.

'This will keep you ready for our next encounter,' he had told her, his voice thick with suppressed excitement. 'You're not to take it off, not even at night. Nor are you to touch yourself – I will know if you've come in my absence. Do you understand, Angel?'

Reacting to the steely note in his voice as he gave that last instruction, Ariane had found herself answering in the affirmative, her voice quivering with tension. Satisfied with her response, Conrad had dressed her lovingly before bringing her home.

That had been hours ago. The light was beginning to fade outside her window and Ariane threw down her pen with disgust. Rising, she winced as the leather strap chafed against her delicate membranes, reactivating the sensitive nerve endings which had been quivering on the brink of climax all day.

Gingerly, she walked into the kitchen to make herself some supper. She had to admit, it was a devilishly clever device Conrad had given her. It kept her in a state of constant arousal, yet didn't quite touch her in such a way that it would tip her over the edge.

Conrad knew what he was doing. Had he given Melissa a chastity belt before he left home? Was she as smitten as Ariane, compelled by her own dark needs to submit to Conrad's every whim?

Thinking of Melissa made Ariane think of Jon. He had mentioned the other girl several times when he phoned her. He hadn't rung today, at least, not while she was here. What was Jon doing now? She pictured him, lonely in his hotel room, and felt a pang of shame.

In his hotel room, Jon was waiting for Melissa. He had spent the day fantasising about the evening ahead, steadfastly ignoring the signals she had been giving out in his office. *Look but don't touch – not too much, anyhow.* Her about-face had confused and annoyed him. It wasn't as if it was a mild flirtation they had enjoyed the night before – she had fellated him to a climax, for God's sake!

He had arranged for room service to serve dinner in his suite, so there would be no possibility of their being interrupted. If this was merely a tease to increase his desire for her, it had worked. Being at the office had been a total waste of time, all his attention had been focused on the evening to come.

At eight precisely, there was a knock at the door. Feeling like an adolescent, unsure of himself in a way he didn't like, Jon adjusted the collar of his denim shirt and went to open the door.

'Hello, Jon.'

Her voice was like smoky whisky and her eyes caressed him as she ran them over his shirt and jeans. He thought he detected a glimmer of approval in her dark eyes as she raised them to his. She smiled, a small, knowing smile that sent a rush of adrenalin surging through his veins.

'Hello, Melissa.'

His voice sounded strange to his own ears, deeper and huskier than normal. He stood aside to let her pass, his eyes following her. He could feel the tension stretching like a thin thread between them, on the verge of snapping.

She was wearing a figure-hugging, cream-coloured top which moulded the firm globes of her breasts, delineating her nipples and the wide areolae surrounding them. There was no ugly line caused by a bra strap and her skin showed, faintly pink, through the pale, clinging fabric.

On her feet, she wore black suede boots which ended just below her knee. The heels were medium height and square, the toes shaped to show off the smallness of her feet. Her legs were bare, tanned a delicious caramel, the flesh soft but well toned. Watching her walk across the room, Jon saw the muscles in the backs of her thighs ripple under their velvety covering and he had an instant image of her strong legs gripping him around the waist as he drove into her.

Aware that his cock had reacted instantly to the visual stimulus, he turned away on the pretext of pouring them both drinks.

'Bourbon?' he suggested.

'I'll wait for the champagne, thank you,' she replied, eyeing the bottle of Moet buried in the ice bucket on the coffee table.

Jon smiled tightly.

'Of course.'

He had to get a grip on himself, regain the control he had sensed he had over the situation before. With Melissa looking at him like that he wasn't sure how to react, and he didn't like the feeling. He felt inexplicably angry with her, as if holding her responsible for his discomfort.

Her skirt was no more than a wide belt of black lycra, barely covering the tender crease between her legs and buttocks. As she sat down on the sofa opposite him, he saw that she was wearing filmy white panties, so snug that the material had burrowed into the cleft of her pink-skinned, shaven sex.

Jon did not comment, though her eyes challenged him. What the hell was she playing at? This morning she had gone out of her way to make it perfectly clear that she was backing off – now it seemed that she had changed her mind. Or had she? Maybe her mouth would still say *don't touch* even while her body screamed *fuck me!*

Their meal arrived: daintily arranged shellfish and warm salad. Melissa ate hungrily, balancing her plate on her lap precariously. She ate with a relish that was almost childlike, using her fingers and concentrating all her attention on her food. When she had finished, she sucked her fingers clean and took a gulp of the champagne Jon had poured for her.

'You were hungry,' he said, watching her.

Melissa grinned, abandoning her empty plate on the coffee table. Leaning back in her seat, she crossed one leg over the other slowly. Jon caught a glimpse of pink and white and felt his mouth run dry. Jesus, what was she trying to do to him?

'It was good. Aren't you hungry?'

Jon glanced down at his barely touched meal and put it aside. The hunger he was experiencing had nothing to do with food, and everything to do with the elusive young woman sitting opposite him.

'Why have you come tonight, Melissa?' he asked her bluntly.

She seemed amused by the question, as if she hadn't expected him to be bold enough to ask it.

'You asked me to,' she pointed out reasonably.

'This morning you told me you couldn't come.'

Melissa leaned forward and picked up her glass. She took a long swallow of champagne before she answered.

'Yes, well, that was before I spoke to Conrad.'

Jon's eyebrows rose. Play it cool, he told himself, don't let her see how she's confusing you.

'Go on,' he said, feigning indifference.

'I told him you wanted to see me. He said to go ahead.' She shrugged. 'So here I am.'

'What if Conrad had told you not to come?'

Melissa held his eye.

'Then I would have had to make a decision.'

'What kind of decision?'

'About whether disobeying Conrad would ultimately bring me more pleasure than doing as he said.' She watched him intently, as if gauging his reaction.

Jon refilled their glasses, giving himself time to consider what she had said.

'What did Conrad tell you to do tonight?'

Melissa smiled slowly.

'He told me that I should turn you on, and make you come any way you, or I, wanted.'

Jon felt his cock swell and pressed his hands into his lap to suppress it.

'Don't I have any say in this?'

'Of course!' Melissa laughed. 'But you must understand – you mustn't penetrate me, at least not with your cock. And I mustn't come. Apart from those two provisos, we can have a ball.'

Jon's eyes widened in disbelief, tinged with fury.

'I'm not in the habit of being told by a girl's lover what I may or may not do with her. I like my women to do what *I* want.'

'Like Ariane?'

Jon felt himself flush.

'Leave Ariane out of this.'

'Why?'

'Because she has nothing to do with you and I. I don't want to discuss my relationship with her with you.' He was seized by a surge of irritation that brought his brows beetling together in a scowl. 'Perhaps you'd better leave, Melissa. I don't think I like the games you're playing.'

Melissa merely smiled at him, calm in the face of his irritation.

'Don't you?' she said softly.

Jon watched through narrowed eyes as she trailed her own fingertips down her chest, her long, red-painted fingernails circling the soft flesh of her areola. Her tongue ran along the inner edge of her lower lip, moistening it, and Jon felt his body respond.

'In England we have a name for girls like you,' he said huskily as she began to pinch and pull at her hardening nipple.

'Yes?' she said breathily, leaning forward so that her soft, full breasts quivered under the thin covering of her top.

'You're a cock-tease, Melissa, and you're playing a dangerous game.'

She laughed, a soft, husky sound that shivered over his senses.

'Oh, good,' she said, squirming lewdly against the supple leather of the sofa. 'My favourite kind!'

Swearing under his breath, Jon heaved the coffee table aside and crouched in front of her. He had a deep, overwhelming desire, not to hurt her, but to subdue her in some way, to convert that knowing, almost mocking look in her eyes into the adoring, submissive gaze she had turned on him before.

He didn't know where the feeling came from, and at that moment, he didn't care. Kneeling on the floor in front of her, he looked up into her face and saw her eyes widen. Sensing her tension, he smiled slightly, running his hands up her lower legs to her knees. The suede of her boots made his skin prickle and he played for a moment with the rim below her knee. Wanting to spin out the tension for as long as possible, he described small circles on the soft skin of her knees, smiling to himself as the tiny hairs on the surface of her skin stood up.

Jon felt hot. This close to her, he could feel the feminine, animal heat of her body, could smell her familiar perfume, and the richer, unmistakable musk of arousal. This evidence that she desired him acted as a spur to his senses, driving him on.

The insides of her thighs felt smooth as silk as he ran his fingertips along them. As he reached the point where the provocative little band of a skirt ended, he splayed his fingers and pressed her legs apart.

He had never seen a shaven quim before, and the sight fascinated him. The skin was smooth and pale, a perfect continuum between her belly and her thighs. He could see the faint sheen of her feminine secretions on the soft pink lips which poked lewdly through the crease and he pushed her legs further apart, wanting to see more.

Her depilated labia parted beneath the inadequate strip of white nylon. Jon frowned as he caught the glint of gold nestling in the folds of flesh.

'What is this?' he asked her, hooking his fingers under the side of the panties and easing them aside.

There was a ring, about the thickness and circumference of a wedding ring, piercing the left labia, just below her clitoris. Glancing up at her face, Jon saw that she was watching him intently, gauging his reaction.

His initial horror gave way to fascination and he tugged gently on the hoop of gold. The effect was immediate; a thin, tiny pearl of moisture gathered at the lip of her vagina, and remained there, glistening.

The hole through her flesh was clean, rather like the holes in Ariane's pierced earlobes, and Jon realised that the operation must have been performed by a professional. On closer examination, he saw that there was another, identical hole on the opposite labia, though this had virtually closed in the absence of a ring.

'Where's the other one?' he asked.

'Conrad took it with him.'

Jon tugged again on the band of gold and Melissa groaned.

'Please, Jon – I mustn't come. Let me touch you—'

'Not yet.'

Jon was startled by the streak of sadistic satisfaction which flashed through him as he saw her anguished expression. It felt good, holding this power over her, and he welcomed the feeling, bringing with it, as it did, that wonderful sense of potency which he had felt before.

On closer examination, he saw that the inner lips had been stretched, so much so that they protruded below the outer labia by at least an inch. Imagining the constant friction as she walked intrigued him.

'How was this done?' he demanded, pulling on the now slippery folds of flesh.

'Weights,' she told him, her breathing shallow, as if she was trying desperately hard to hold on to her self-control.

Yet, he noticed, she made no attempt to close her legs, or pull away from him.

'*Weights*?' he echoed.

'Yes. Conrad attaches little weights to the rings . . . it pulls the lips and trains them to hang down . . . where he can always get at them. Sometimes he attaches a fine chain with a loop at the other end which he wears over his ring finger . . . Ohh!'

While she was speaking, Jon was playing with the ring, fascinated by her responses. He imagined leading her around by the labia, having this sensitive, most intimate part of her attached to him and felt a rush of desire to his loins.

Before she could protest, he buried his face between her thighs and breathed in the musky, feminine scent of her. Melissa gasped, her thigh muscles contracting around his head as he toyed with the gold ring with his tongue. Jon used his hands to push her legs further apart, licking gently along the channels of her sex and flicking his tongue across her burgeoning clitoris.

'Please . . . no!' she gasped, tangling her fingers in his hair and trying to lift his head away from her.

Jon looked up, noting her flushed face and the glazed expression in her eyes. The dew of her arousal was heavy on his tongue and he wanted more, much more.

He smiled cruelly, enjoying the way her eyes widened as she read his expression.

'We have to obey the rules,' she told him, her voice quivering with emotion. 'You don't understand.'

'Explain to me, then. What is this hold Conrad has over you that makes you do exactly as he tells you?'

Melissa's face took on a misty, dreamy look that surprised him.

'Conrad is . . . like the other half of me. His pleasure is my pleasure and I would do anything to increase it.' She looked at him steadily, her eyes willing him to understand what she was trying to say. 'I'm his willing slave.'

'And if you disobey him?'

Melissa shook her head.

'I won't disobey Conrad,' she said emphatically.

'Won't you?' Jon said, smiling. 'We'll see. Conrad's "rules" are not mine to obey, only you are bound by them. Now – why don't we have some more champagne?'

Sitting back on the opposite sofa, Jon watched her face. He recognised the flicker of alarm that she hid, too late, and felt a thrill rush through him. By the end of the evening he would make sure she had broken every one of Conrad's rules. Raising his glass to her, he toasted her silently, confident that by the time she left his hotel room, Melissa would have a new master.

# *Six*

Ariane lay wakeful in the bed she normally shared with Jon and stared at the shadows dancing on the ceiling. The bed seemed cold and wide without him in it and she felt restless and insecure. Underneath her nightdress, the leather strap that Conrad had fastened round her forced her to focus all her attention on the moist, over-sensitised flesh between her thighs.

How did Conrad expect her to remain in such a heightened sense of anticipation until he returned, when it would be a simple matter to put her hands between her legs and stroke the straining bud at the apex of her labia? It would give her such relief to be able to climax; maybe it would even help her to sleep.

Jon still hadn't phoned. It wasn't like him, and the fact that he'd missed a day worried her. She had the number for his hotel, and she toyed with the idea of ringing him. It was strange, but her absorption with Conrad in no way diminished her feelings for Jon, and she longed to talk to him, to share her frustration with him, even though he knew she could not tell him what was happening to her.

There was nothing to stop her ringing him, though. Impulsively, she picked up the telephone and dialled long distance. Ariane's heart leapt when the connection was made and she heard

his familiar, well-loved voice on the other end of the telephone
wire.

'Jon? It's me – Ariane.'

'Sweetheart! It's lovely to hear your voice,' he said, his voice
low, caressing her ear as he spoke.

'You didn't ring today, darling – I was worried,' she admitted,
settling herself more comfortably against the pillows.

'I'm sorry, Ariane – the day was just so packed. What time is
it there?'

Ariane glanced at the bedside clock.

'Eleven-thirty. I'm in bed, but I can't sleep.'

'Why can't you sleep, sweetheart? Everything's okay, isn't
it?'

'Yes, yes of course,' she replied, reassuring him hurriedly.

'Thank God for that! I don't like to think of you being on your
own. I miss you, sweetheart.'

Ariane closed her eyes and hugged the phone close.

'Oh Jon, I'm so glad to hear you say that,' she admitted. 'I
can't sleep because the bed's too big without you . . . and cold,
too.'

'I know, darling.'

'And I'm feeling so . . . you know . . . so *horny* – I wish you
were here!'

There was a short, shocked silence at the other end of the line
and Ariane bit her lip. She never spoke like that to Jon, he must
be wondering what had come over her. When he replied, although
his words weren't quite what she had hoped for, she was relieved
to hear that his voice had dropped a pitch, and he appeared to be
pleased with what she had said.

'I wish I was there too, sweetheart,' he admitted.

Ariane took a deep breath and pushed her luck.

'If . . . if you *were* here, Jon, what would you do?'

'What would I do? I'd hold you, darling, and whisper sweet nothings in your ear.'

Ariane felt a surge of frustration. That wasn't what she wanted to hear.

'That wouldn't cure my horniness, though, would it?' she said, holding her breath as she waited for his response.

'Are you feeling all right, Ariane?' he asked her after a few moments.

'Not really. I'm hot and restless and I've got this ache, low down in my stomach . . . I want you, Jon. Does that shock you?'

'Shock me? No, sweetheart, it doesn't shock me. How could it? I'm flattered, of course, and I wish more than ever I could be there with you . . .'

'What would you do if you were?' Ariane repeated her earlier question, pressing the heel of her hand against her mons in a vain attempt to release some of the pressure which was building, tormenting her. 'Please, Jon – I need you to talk to me.'

He didn't refuse, but he sounded uncomfortable as he told her.

'I'd . . . kiss you, and touch you . . .'

'My breasts – would you touch my breasts?' she prompted desperately, running her own fingertips back and forth across her aching nipples.

'Of course – you know how I love your breasts!'

'Would . . . would you suck them and kiss them?'

'Ariane—'

'*Please*, Jon.'

'You know I would. I'd kiss from your neck, down between your breasts. Your skin is so soft there. Then I'd hold you close . . .'

89

'And?'

She felt desperate, wanting him to be more specific, to feed the desire which had been churning through her veins all day, to help her release it.

'And I'd love you, sweetheart. Isn't that what you want – to be loved?'

'I want . . . I want to be *cherished*,' she said, her voice aching with need.

'Well, I'd do that too, sweetheart. Love you and cherish you. Always.'

Though his words were romantic and loving, they were not specific enough for Ariane. She wanted him to be explicit, to tip her over the edge with words as Conrad had done when he telephoned her after their first encounter. She moaned slightly, just loudly enough to cause Jon concern.

'Ariane? Are you all right, darling?'

She smiled faintly.

'Yes, I'm fine. Like I said before, I'm missing you. This bed is awfully lonely . . . sex is awfully lonely without you.'

'Save it for me, sweetheart,' he said.

'I don't know if I can.'

Did the idea of her masturbating shock him? It was not something that they had ever discussed and she guessed that her mention of it, however oblique, had thrown him. Then she heard something else, another voice in the background and she froze, mortified that she had been opening her heart to him when someone else was there.

'Is there someone there with you?' she said.

'Just someone from the office,' Jon replied smoothly.

'Oh. You should have said you weren't alone, I wouldn't have kept you so long on the phone.'

She felt embarrassed now, and rather foolish.

'You know I'd rather talk to you than anyone else,' he told her, his voice low and reassuring. 'I'd better go now though, sweetheart. You try to get some sleep – I'll call you tomorrow.'

'All right.'

'Goodnight.'

'Goodnight, Jon. I love you.'

'I love you too, sweetheart,' he said, then the line went dead.

Replacing the receiver gently on its cradle, Ariane was left feeling even more restless and lonely. Sliding her fingers down, between her legs, she touched herself gently. Her conversation with Jon, unsatisfactory though it had been, had fuelled her arousal and, barely knowing what she was doing, she began to strum gently on the hard little bead of her clitoris.

Closing her eyes, Ariane welcomed the warmth spreading slowly through her body, knowing that a climax would help her to sleep. It wasn't as if Conrad would ever know and, after all, it was her body. If she wanted to masturbate, that was her choice.

*Except that she had agreed to play by the rules of the game*, a small, dissenting voice reminded her. *Shut up*, another voice said, focusing on the ripples of pleasure radiating out from the centre of her, growing stronger and warmer by the minute.

In her mind's eye, she imagined that Jon was with her, that it was his hand burrowing into the feminine, wet heat between her thighs, his fingertips playing on the pulsing tip of her clitoris. She imagined she felt his mouth enclose her breast, his teeth tugging at her aching nipple far more roughly than he would ever tug at it in real life.

Suddenly, in her imagination, his hands and mouth became rougher, more bruising, wringing the pleasure from her rather than coaxing it, forcing her to the point of no return. The leather strap chafed against the slippery folds of her flesh as she thrashed about on the bed, her hand curling into her body as her orgasm crested and broke.

'Jon!' she cried, bucking her hips off the bed and imagining him burying his face in the scented folds of her sex as it convulsed with pleasure. 'Oh God, Jon – come home! Come home to me!'

She collapsed, panting against the pillows. Her hand was wet with her own dew and her breasts and sex throbbed with exhaustion. Slowly, she realised that, somehow, Conrad would know that she had disobeyed him. There would be a reckoning for these few moments of madness.

Curling into a ball, she pulled the covers around her and pressed her hand sleepily between her legs. The flesh still pulsed gently and she wriggled to make herself more comfortable. And she knew, in a flash of mental clarity that, for all that she loved Jon, she couldn't wait for the day of reckoning with Conrad to come.

Putting the telephone down after Ariane's call, Jon frowned at it, still shaken by the tone of her voice. It hadn't sounded like Ariane. She had seemed . . . desperate, restless, quite unlike herself.

Feeling Melissa's eyes on him, he looked across at her and smiled.

'Sorry about that. I didn't call Ariane as arranged and she was worried.'

'Is she lonely without you?'

'Are you lonely without Conrad?' he countered at once.

'Touché,' she said, smiling. 'Doesn't it occur to you that Ariane might well be amusing herself in your absence in the same way that you are?'

She laughed softly at his shocked expression.

'Absolutely not,' Jon said firmly. 'Ariane is strictly a one-man woman – she wouldn't dream of being unfaithful to me.'

'Isn't she even feeling a little . . . *frustrated*?'

Jon thought of Ariane's odd tone, her near desperation as she had tried to get him to talk dirty to her and he frowned.

'Of course not,' he said unconvincingly.

Ariane had virtually come right out and said that she was masturbating . . . the idea of it made him feel hot and restless. Briefly, he imagined Ariane sitting where Melissa was sitting, wearing Melissa's clothes. In his mind's eye, he imagined doing to her the things he was planning to do to Melissa, and he had an instant erection.

No! Ariane was a different kind of woman, how could he think such things about her?

'It seems to me,' Melissa said, breaking into his thoughts with uncanny prescience, 'that you have the unfortunate habit of dividing women into madonnas and whores. Ariane has fulfilled the madonna role quite satisfactorily for you – now you've found your whore.'

'Is that what you are, Melissa – a whore?'

She smiled enigmatically at him.

'That depends on your point of view.' Rising from the sofa, she bent down and brushed her smooth, soft-skinned cheek briefly against his. 'But can you be absolutely sure that there isn't a bit of the whore in your madonna that you just haven't noticed?'

Jon caught her at the back of her neck and twisted her head round so that she was forced to look at him.

'Don't talk about Ariane that way. Ariane has nothing to do with what happens here, between you and I. If you've come tonight as a whore, then let's start on the business.'

Unfazed by his brusque demand, Melissa smiled into his eyes.

'I thought you'd never ask,' she said. 'Where do you want me?'

Jon stared at her, so beautiful in her hooker's clothes, handing herself to him on a plate. How far would she go in the name of obedience to Conrad? What would it take to make her come against her will?

'Take your pants off,' he said, making no move to rise from his seat. 'I want to see your cunt.'

If he had hoped to get some reaction from her with his crudeness, he was disappointed. Melissa merely reached under her short skirt and wriggled out of the wisp of fabric which passed for panties and handed them to him. They were damp, impregnated with the exotic, musky scent of her arousal. Passing them under his nose, Jon inhaled deeply before casting them aside.

There was a small dining table by the window, with a highly polished surface and a single pedestal.

'Lay across the table,' he told her.

Christ, she was like a Stepford Wife, reacting to his every whim as if she had no will of her own. Jon watched as she leaned across the table, her soft breasts pressing against the hard, unyielding surface, her skirt riding up to reveal her bare bottom and the pink, shiny purse of her sex between her legs.

'Slide your feet apart,' he said, aware that his voice had grown hoarse.

Melissa complied and the gold ring was revealed once more, together with an unexpected mark on the inside of one buttock.

'What's this?' he asked, going over to investigate.

'Conrad's mark,' she said simply.

She quivered as Jon traced the outline of the tattooed 'C' with his fingertip. She'd allowed someone to tattoo her *here*? Inexplicably, he imagined opening Ariane's pert, rounded bottom to reveal his own initial tattooed in the folds and his cock pressed painfully against the front of his jeans.

Christ, why couldn't he get Ariane out of his head? Maybe it was her phone call that had pushed her to the forefront of his consciousness. Whatever it was, he was aware that every time he looked at Melissa, he was reminded of the woman he had left at home.

If it was Ariane lying here in front of him now, he would ask her what she wanted, let her decide how they should proceed.

'What would Conrad do to you now?' he asked.

Melissa looked round, clearly surprised by his question.

'He'd punish me,' she said, caught off guard.

'*Punish* you? For what?'

'For teasing him all day.'

Jon felt hot and, somehow, it seemed difficult to breathe. Melissa's words had crystallised the half-formed desires which had plagued him since he met her. More than anything he wanted to *punish* her, punish her until she was crazed with desire, begging him to stop.

Tentatively, he reached out and laid his hand on the cool, smooth skin of her bottom. He saw her shiver and knew that he had found the key.

'I'd like to punish you, Melissa,' he said, his voice shaking slightly. 'I'd like to turn this white skin pink, I'd like to thrash you so hard you won't be able to sit down.'

'Oh, yes,' she breathed.

For a moment, Jon was at a loss. He could use his hand to spank her, but somehow he knew instinctively that that wouldn't be enough, for either of them. As if sensing his hesitation, Melissa whispered, 'Use your belt.'

Perversely, now that he had the answer to his dilemma, Jon felt the need to reassert himself.

'All in good time,' he said, leaning over her back and kneading her breasts through the soft fabric of her top.

'How do you stop yourself from coming, Melissa,' he said softly, his fingertips pressing against the hard, shiny buttons of her nipples.

'I think of Conrad,' she said, her voice cracking with emotion as he pinched her tender flesh, rolling the nipples between his fingers and thumbs until she quivered with pleasure.

'Are you thinking of Conrad now?'

'Yes.'

Leaning forward, he tugged gently on the lobe of her ear with his teeth. Tracing the whorls of her ear with his tongue, he blew softly into her ear, his voice sighing across her senses.

'And now?'

'Yes,' she whispered, though with less conviction than before.

Smiling to himself, Jon straightened. The shape of her upturned bottom fascinated him, and he stroked his palm rhythmically across the pale skin, making her sigh with pleasure.

'So soft,' he said, half to himself.

Her skin was warm beneath his hand, her flesh soft and springy. Tiny, fine hairs furred the surface so that it looked like a ripe peach. Curling his fingers between her thighs, Jon sought the warm, pulpy interior of her sex, feeling the viscous, sweet juices coating his fingers as he caressed the slippery folds of skin.

Her clitoris had slipped from beneath its protective hood and it quivered as he passed his fingertips lightly over the head.

'Please . . . don't!' she moaned.

Jon smiled to himself, confident that the plea was merely part of the script she – or Conrad – had written for her to perform. He wondered how firmly Melissa believed in her ability to remain unmoved by what they were doing together. Conrad must have set her up to fail – with or without her complicity? Whatever, Jon knew he would enjoy making her come, supposedly against her will.

Now, though, he had other, more urgent needs of his own to explore. Bringing back his hand, he slapped her, hard, across the buttocks. The sound of flesh against flesh was loud in the room and he repeated the action, watching the way her soft, white skin suffused with colour.

He'd never spanked a woman before, though he recognised now that he had often felt the urge. Melissa merely gasped as he slapped her again, and he was seized by a shocking, urgent need to provoke a stronger reaction from her. *Use your belt* she had said. It wasn't quite right for what he wanted, but he unbuckled it none the less.

Melissa stiffened as she recognised the sound of the leather being drawn through the denim belt loops and he smiled to himself. He wouldn't give her what she expected, at least, not yet.

Casting around the room for something else to use, Jon's gaze fell on the telephone. The flex which connected the telephone to the socket was disconnectable at both ends. Pulling it out, Jon doubled the flex so that the hard little plastic connectors were both in his hand and he was left with a long loop of flex.

Melissa cried out in surprise as the first stinging blow landed across her unsuspecting buttocks.

'Oh God!' she cried as he whipped her again and again, turning her skin from pale rose to a deep, fiery red.

'Please, please, no more!' she gasped.

Jon paused, unable to drag his eyes away from the stripes

which criss-crossed her skin from the backs of her legs to the top of her crease. Dropping the flex, he laid one hand on each buttock. The heat seared his palms, sending a surge of lust to his loins, equal to the pang of guilt which shot through him as he realised how heavily she was breathing. As if each ragged breath caused her pain. Had he hurt her?

Melissa was panting, her legs quivering as she struggled to maintain her position. Opening her buttocks as if parting two halves of a ripe fruit, Jon saw that her sex was swollen and wet. He knew then that she had derived as much pleasure as he from the whipping. Her clitoris was so swollen he could see it glistening at the apex of her labia. How long could she hold out?

'You love it, don't you?' he said, his voice unrecognisable as he unfastened his jeans, seeking to relieve some of the pressure on his cock.

*You can't fuck me*, she had said. If he made her come, would that proviso be forgotten too?

'Yes, I love it,' she admitted breathily. 'We have to stop now, I—'

'Just a minute,' he said, putting a hand at the small of her back to stop her from rising. 'You asked me to use my belt – remember?'

'Oh!'

Picking the belt up from where he had dropped it on the floor, Jon draped it teasingly over the burning flesh of her bottom. Melissa moaned and wriggled her hips, as if trying to escape the warm kiss of the leather.

Acting on instinct, Jon trailed the tip of the belt between her legs, flicking it gently against the delicate flesh on the insides of her thighs. Melissa sucked in her breath, her whole body held taut, waiting to see what he would do next.

'I'm going to make you come, Melissa,' he said softly, allowing the belt to beat gently against her swollen labia.

'No!' she cried brokenly. 'I can't . . .'

'You will. I can sense your climax building. You're so wet, so willing. I'll tell Conrad that, shall I? Tell him how willing you were to break his rules?'

'No! Oh, no! Oh!'

Jon flicked the tip of the belt once, twice, three times against the quivering protuberance of her clitoris. Each stinging little pain pushed her farther and farther towards the point of no return. Just before she tipped over, he pushed two fingers into her wetness and smeared the fluid across the entrance to her rectum.

'Conrad says I can't fuck you. Did he say anything about buggery?'

He heard Melissa's sharp intake of breath and sensed the moment that she finally submitted to him. He smacked her hard on the clitoris with the end of his leather belt and she came at once, arching her back and voicing defeat with an anguished cry.

'Yes,' she screamed, reaching behind her and dragging her buttocks apart. 'Fuck my arse, Jon – fuck it now!'

Jon didn't need any further invitation. Lubricating her thoroughly with a combination of her own copious juices and the fluid seeping from his cock, he pushed against the puckered rim, gritting his teeth against the resistance he encountered.

'Come on, baby,' he coaxed, holding her as wide apart as he could, 'let me in now . . . open up, for me.'

He felt her bear down and at once the portal was breached. Slowly, he inched his way inside her, feeling the strong, dry walls of her back passage press against the intrusion. It was so hot, so tight, *so good*. He began to tremble, aware of the ejaculate gathering at the base of his balls.

The heat of her abused bottom pressed against him and the memory of whipping her fuelled his desire, making him pump his hips back and forth. His own body seemed to absorb the heat, every nerve ending quivering with heightened sensitivity as he moved inside her. The pressure was building inside his head, the blood pumping, pressing behind his eyeballs until he felt his head would explode.

Melissa reached between her own legs and entered herself with two fingers. Jon could feel her caressing his cock through her own thin membranes and the sensation drove him wild.

'I'm going to come,' he breathed as she stroked him. 'Jesus . . . ah!'

It jetted out of him, filling her rectum and seeping out to coat his balls and belly. He pulled out of her sharply and the last, almost painful spurts spattered over her burning buttocks. Jon massaged his semen into her flesh as if it were a cooling balm, and Melissa moaned.

Slowly, he turned her in his arms and scanned her face. She was crying softly, though her eyes glowed and her soft mouth trembled, her lips parting eagerly under his as he kissed her.

'It's all right, baby,' he told her, holding her close and stroking her face. 'You belong to me, too, now – it's going to be okay.'

'But, Conrad—'

'Will understand. He has no choice. While I am here you will submit to me. No one else exists – just you and I.'

He held her eye, watched and absorbed the brief inner struggle apparent in her expressive eyes. Then she nodded, and Jon felt himself stir once more as he thought of the possibilities which lay before him.

The few short weeks of his secondment had taken on the guise of a period out of time, like a small, turbulent tidal wave in the normally serene waters of his life. Jon had a sense of something momentous happening to him and he revelled in it, sure that he was on the path to true self-fulfilment – all with the help of the beautiful young woman who clung to him now, her eyes telling him more clearly than any words could that she was his, for as long as he wanted her to be.

For a moment he wondered which of them had the true power – the dominant or the submissive? Something clicked in his chest as he realised he was as much in her thrall as she was in his. For an instant he felt claustrophobic as he realised that he, too, was trapped. Then Melissa smiled at him, and he relaxed, confident that the trap was lined with silk.

# *Seven*

The hours passed with excruciating slowness for Ariane as she waited for Conrad to contact her. She worked diligently at her drawing board, but, no matter how hard she tried, she found she could not concentrate on the project in hand. Instead, she found herself doodling on the edges of the paper, creating brief, fluent line-drawings of herself as she imagined Conrad must see her.

Gradually, Ariane abandoned her commissioned work, and indulged herself. Before long, she had built up a respectable portfolio of what she supposed could only be described as erotic art.

In between, she prepared meals, slept and spoke to Jon daily on the telephone. Jon sounded vague and distracted and their conversations were brief. No less loving than usual, but unsatisfactory in a way Ariane could not quite explain.

Perhaps it was that he sounded rather like she felt, and that exacerbated her own restlessness. Did he notice the difference in her? Normally they were so in tune with one another and it worried her that now there were secrets between them. Nothing, though, not even her fears for her relationship with Jon, could stop her from thinking constantly of Conrad.

His was the face which invaded her dreams, his the voice which implanted erotic images in her mind as she stroked and caressed herself. The leather strap fastened between her legs served as a constant reminder of his instructions, underlining her guilt even whilst tinting it with a delicious, illicit glow. The strap chafed her delicate skin as she walked to the corner shop, it tormented the base of her clitoris when she moved until she was distracted to the point of insanity.

On the third day since she had seen Conrad, Ariane had lunch with her agent. Frank Nimmoy was an old and dear friend who had been at school with Ariane's father, and their regular monthly lunch date was always something to which she looked forward with pleasure.

Today, though, she found she couldn't sit still, wriggling on the scratchy surface of her seat in the restaurant until her vulva burned and throbbed with need.

'Are you all right?' Frank asked her as she lost the thread of their conversation for the third time.

Ariane stared at him, the blood zinging through her veins, her limbs warm and heavy, and shook her head.

'I'm sorry,' she said. 'Would you excuse me for a minute?'

Trying to ignore the concern in his eyes, she took herself off to the ladies. Secreting herself in a cubicle, she locked the door and pulled her panties down to her knees. Slipping one foot through so that they dangled from one ankle, she spread her legs, pressing one foot against the cubicle wall, the other against the floor.

Her open sex was hot and wet and hungry. Ariane's fingers sank into the warm, pulpy flesh, slipping under the strap to find the entrance to her body. The pleated walls of her vagina sucked at her fingers, contracting around them as, with her other hand, she rubbed her aching clitoris.

The smooth leather of the split strap which fitted along the channels of flesh either side of her labia, had been softened by her juices, the slippery surface feeling like another ridge of her skin. Ariane caressed it as much as she stroked the rest of herself, loving Conrad for leaving her wearing it, so that she could not forget him during these most intimate moments.

Within minutes, she brought herself to a shuddering climax, sitting, legs akimbo, on the toilet bowl.

Afterwards, she felt dirty and ashamed, but even these emotions aroused her. Staring at her face in the unkindly lit mirror above the washbasin, she gazed at her flushed cheeks, her overbright eyes and despaired.

'What have you woken in me, Conrad?' she whispered to her dishevelled image. 'Night and day – I can think of nothing but sex! There's no room to live my life.'

Even now, after she had readjusted the leather strap and splashed her face with cold water, she could feel the first tendrils of desire curling in her belly. It was always the same – no matter how deep and satisfying her climax, it was never enough, never sufficient to quiet her clamorous senses.

Frank's eyes scanned her worriedly as she came back to the table.

'Are you sure you're all right, dear?' he asked her as she sat opposite him again.

'I am a little under the weather,' she said, hating herself for lying to him, yet knowing she had no choice.

At once he was solicitous, ordering her a taxi and insisting that she should return home at once. They waited inside the restaurant, drinking coffee and making small talk. Ariane was aware that Frank's eyes rested on her with concern and she was embarrassed to have caused him so much anxiety. What would he think if he knew the real cause of her agitation?

'Ah, here we are,' he said suddenly.

Looking up, Ariane saw a young man wearing tight-fitting jeans and a pale chambray shirt approaching the table. He was tall and well-built, his face square and tanned with an attractive cleft denting his chin. His clean, dirty-blond hair was cropped attractively short, moulding the contours of his skull.

'Taxi for Nimmoy?' he said, his accent pure cockney, his voice husky as only a heavy smoker's can be.

Though his query was directed at Frank, his gaze rested on Ariane and she felt herself grow warm under his steady regard. If other men had noticed her while she had been living with Jon, she hadn't noticed it, but now, for the first time, she welcomed the admiration of someone new. Especially someone as obviously virile as this man.

'It's for the young lady, actually,' Frank was saying. 'She's not feeling too well, so I'd like you to make sure she gets in safely.'

He peeled a ten pound note from a roll which he took from his pocket and handed it to the driver.

'For your trouble,' he said, then, peeling off two more he added, 'that should cover the fare. Ariane?'

Ariane started and, dragging her eyes away from the driver's she saw that Frank had seen the attraction between them and was looking quizzically at her. Feeling the heat seep into her cheeks, she avoided his eye as she bent to pick up her bag.

'Thanks, Frank,' she said, pressing her lips against his cheek.

His skin was dry and warm and, breathing in the familiar scent of him, Ariane wondered what it would be like to make love to someone so much older than her. Surely experience would compensate for the lower stamina which came with age? From what she knew of his personality, she was willing to bet that Frank would be a considerate lover, sensual and passionate—

106

'Ariane?'

She jumped and saw that he was watching her, a strange expression on his face. Could he read her mind? Lord, what was the matter with her? She had known Frank since she was a baby, he was like a second father to her. Thinking of him in that way was close to incest!

Disgusted with herself and her virtually uncontrollable urges, Ariane gave him a weak smile and preceded the young cabbie out of the restaurant and into the street. Frank followed them.

'I'll send the contract for you to sign as soon as all the details have been agreed. Take care of yourself now – you'll need plenty of energy for the new job!'

Sinking into the seat in the back of the taxi, Ariane closed her eyes. Frank had negotiated for her the kind of deal that should have her walking on air. It was what she had worked towards ever since she took the plunge and went freelance. So why was the victory like ashes in her mouth?

*Because the one thing you want, you can't have.* The inner voice echoed in her head, taunting her. She knew that it was right – she wanted Conrad. The more he denied her access to his body, the more she wanted it and no amount of masturbation could assuage the need. It made everything else feel unimportant, insignificant in a way she had never thought possible.

'Here we are, love.'

Ariane opened her eyes with a start as the cabbie spoke and she realised she was home already. Meeting his gaze in the driving mirror, she wondered how long he had been watching her. It gave her a thrill to think that she had been unaware of his scrutiny. Had her thoughts been written across her face? His eyes were a deep, sapphire blue and his gaze did not waver as she stared at him.

'Would you mind walking with me to my door – I still feel a bit shaky,' she asked him, never breaking eye-contact.

His eyes crinkled at the corners, so she guessed that he was smiling.

'No problem. I'll just park the cab somewhere legal.'

Ariane watched the play of his shoulder muscles under the chambray shirt as he manoeuvred into a parking space outside the block of flats. Running her eyes up his neck, she found she liked the way the small hairs at his nape formed an orderly 'vee' on either side of a central line. His hair was naturally lighter at the ends, as if he spent a lot of time in the sun. It was shaped around his ears, which were neat and well-shaped, lying flat against his skull.

Killing the engine, he turned in his seat and met her eyes directly for the first time.

'Which floor?' he asked.

Ariane smiled slowly, relishing the low pulse of desire which beat in her lower belly.

'I'll show you,' she said.

Climbing out of the cab, he opened the door for her. Ariane caught the scent of his skin as she stepped out onto the pavement. It smelled clean and masculine with a hint of citrus-scented toiletries and she felt her mouth and throat run dry. This had never happened to her before. She'd never wanted a total stranger with such intensity, certainly never wanted a man badly enough to go all out to get what she wanted.

And that was what she intended to do. It barely crossed her mind that he might object – by agreeing to take her upstairs, he had entered into the contract. Glancing at him, Ariane saw the slight swagger in his walk, the glint in his eye that told her he couldn't quite believe his luck, and she smiled to herself. He didn't know what he had let himself in for! Here was a man who had nothing to do with Conrad, or Jon, nor even Ariane herself after this afternoon. He was the perfect, anonymous lover, and she intended to have him in all the ways she could not have Conrad until her desire was satisfied beyond a doubt. Surely that would give her some relief?

Pressing the button in the lift, Ariane turned and eyed him lasciviously.

'Your name is Ariane, isn't it?' he asked her.

She smiled, remembering the day she had met Conrad for the first time. *What need have we of names?*

'It doesn't matter,' she told him. 'Please – don't tell me yours.'

He looked at her uncertainly, and she realised that he was thinking that maybe he had misread the signals she had been giving him, that perhaps she really did want him to deliver her safely to her door, full stop. To reassure him, as soon as the lift arrived and they had stepped inside, Ariane curled her fingers into the open edges of his shirt and pulled him towards her.

His chest was hard and unyielding as she pressed herself against him. She could feel his heart beating thunderously against her breast and the warmth of his skin through his shirt sent little shivers of pleasure through her. His initial surprise at the way she had pulled him against her gave her seconds in which to familiarise herself with the shape of his body, feeling its imprint against hers, so potently masculine it took her breath away.

He was not the sort of man who was content to leave her to take the initiative for long, though. As the lift began to move upward, he tangled his fingers in her hair and, easing her head back, covered her mouth with his. His lips were firm and well-moulded, his skin soft and sensitive. Instead of trying to force his tongue between her teeth as she had half expected him to do, he displayed a finesse that thrilled her.

Though the pressure of his mouth was demanding, the way he licked and nipped at the soft skin of her lower lip delighted her, making her open her mouth willingly under his as she reached up and folded her arms around his neck. Feeling the length of his body pressed boldly against hers, she realised that he was swiftly becoming as aroused as she, and she moved her hips to stimulate the long, hard shaft pressing up against the seam of his jeans.

The lift stopped, too soon, and they were forced to break apart, to step out into the hallway and cross the head of the stairs to Ariane's flat. Reaching into her bag for her keys, Ariane looked up quizzically as he put a restraining hand on her arm.

'My name is Brad,' he said, his eyes a bright, blazing blue, boring into her. 'I want you to use my name.'

Ariane frowned, not liking the way he had swept aside her desire for total anonymity. But if it was so important to him – what the hell? She smiled, slowly.

'How do you do – Brad,' she said, holding out her hand in a small, mockingly formal gesture.

He did not reply, but caught her hand in his. Twisting it over slightly, he bent his head and pressed his warm lips against the inside of her arm, just above her wrist. Ariane shivered as he brushed his lips lightly across the delicate, pale skin, to the crook of her elbow.

Looking up at her, he saw her reaction and his eyes darkened. Without a word, he covered her hand with his and guided the key into the lock. Together they turned it and pushed open the door. As soon as it swung to a close behind them, Ariane pulled Brad against her again and started to kiss him.

She felt feverish, kissing him as if afraid that he would disappear into thin air if her lips, or hands weren't touching him, all the time. Brad seemed to catch her mood of urgency. His hands roamed her back, shaping the smooth indentation of her waist and moulding her hips and buttocks with his palms.

Ariane's lips found the warm triangle of exposed flesh at the opening to his shirt and she closed her eyes, breathing in the warm man-scent of him. Her fingers fumbled with the small buttons, desperate now to feel his bare skin against hers. His hands were pushing under her skirt now, caressing the outsides of her naked thighs, edging towards the elastic of her panties. In a moment he would breach the flimsy barrier and make contact with the slippery, sensitive flesh of her sex, he would touch the moist leather of the strap and—

'Just a minute.'

She pulled away from him as she imagined his reaction to finding the chastity belt she wore.

'Go into the living room . . . I need . . . I won't be a moment. Make yourself . . . comfortable,' she added, eyeing the gratifying bulge in his jeans.

Brad grinned as he followed the line of her gaze. 'Don't be long,' he said, kissing her lingeringly on the lips as he went into the living room.

Ariane went to the bathroom and unfastened the belt. She had worn it around her waist, night and day, ever since Conrad had left. Peeling the strap away from the swollen folds of flesh between her legs, she hid it away in the drawer where she kept her fresh towels.

It felt odd, after wearing the belt constantly for the past few days, to be without it. Having removed her panties in order to take off the belt, she decided to leave them off, and she felt very exposed without the now familiar snug fit around her labia of the soft leather strap. Smoothing her skirt down over her thighs, she went to join Brad in the living room.

He was standing by the window, his hands thrust deeply into the pockets of his jeans, stretching the heavy denim tightly across the tumescence at his groin. His eyes darkened as Ariane walked towards him. She could feel the tension lengthening between them, drawing her forward, like a thread of elastic.

Standing toe to toe with him, she ran her eyes over his face, absorbing his rough-hewn, wholly masculine beauty and prolonging the moment when they would touch, knowing that when they did, there would be no time for such simple pleasures. She felt as though she was poised on the brink of something animal, compelling. The idea excited her, drove her on to make the first move.

Reaching for him, she pulled his shirt out of the waistband of his jeans and unfastened the rest of the buttons. Parting the two halves of his shirt as if unwrapping a Christmas present, she placed her palms squarely on his pectorals, absorbing the heat of his skin and the steady, heavy thump of his heartbeat.

He had a well-muscled chest, sparsely haired and tanned. At the base of his ribs, his torso tapered into a neat waist, his stomach muscles cut and ripped to form a perfect pattern of squares, spoiled only by the sharp indentation of his navel.

He drew a ragged breath as Ariane pressed the tip of her forefinger into his navel and moved it around. With what sounded like a growl, deep in his throat, he caught hold of her hands and brought them up to trap them between his chest and hers. His hard mouth sought hers and he kissed her, more urgently this time, his tongue probing the soft recesses of her mouth, making her quiver with desire.

Moving away from her, his eyes passed across her body in sensual appreciation. Ariane felt her breasts swell, her nipples puckering in response to the intensity of his gaze, and she stood proudly before him, liberated by his admiration.

Curling her fingers under the hemline of her dress, she held his eye as she pulled it slowly up her thighs and over her hips, exposing her naked mound and stomach and her lace covered breasts as she pulled it over her head. Brad leaned forward and helped her out of her bra so that she stood naked before him.

His eyes settled on her depilated vulva. Ariane could see he was fascinated by the sight of her pink, moisture-slick labia poking through the outer lips of her sex and she slid her feet apart slowly to give him a better view.

'Jesus,' he murmured as her sex-lips peeled apart and her distended clitoris was revealed.

Sinking to his knees in front of her, he buried his face in her quim and inhaled deeply. His large hands splayed across her buttocks, pulling her hard against his face as he began to lick and nibble at her sensitive flesh.

Ariane moaned as he touched her clitoris with the tip of his tongue and it quivered hungrily in response. She could feel the warmth spreading through her already as he licked the tiny bud, sucking it gently into his mouth and rolling it on his tongue. Bending her knees, she bore down on his face, pressing her clitoris against his tongue until, at last, she came. A wave of sensation rolled over her, so intense it made her legs buckle and she sank down onto her knees on the carpet beside him. Seeking blindly for his mouth, she licked her own secretions from his chin and lips, kissing him deeply as he pulled her into his arms.

Slowly, as if choreographed, they lay down on the soft pile. Brad's hand caressed her thighs, sweeping upwards to knead and stroke her breasts. Ariane moaned as he sucked one tumescent nipple into his mouth and drew on it deeply, prolonging the aftershocks of orgasm until she was left with a warm, delicious glow which lingered long after her climax had finally ebbed away.

Murmuring words of appreciation and encouragement, she shaped his skull with her hands, enjoying the feel of him under her hands. More than anything, she wanted to feel him inside her, fucking her. When he came up to kiss her face, Ariane reached down to release the erection he had sustained for the past half an hour.

As it sprang into her hand, his penis felt firm and silky, satisfyingly long with an endearing upward curve. Deprived for so long of the pleasure of touching and tasting a male body, Ariane immediately felt her desire rekindle. He did not object when she slid down the length of his body and opened her mouth around the bulbous head of his cock.

Her tongue flicked along the tiny eye which wept copious, salty tears into her mouth. Drawing him in, she reached between his legs to caress his balls, stroking the skin which was taut and firm, full of ejaculate. After a few moments, he shivered and pulled her up to face him.

'I don't want to come in your mouth,' he told her candidly. 'Will you take it from behind?'

She would have 'taken it' any which way, had he but known, for by now Ariane felt that her entire body was vibrating with need, every nerve ending quivering with a desire denied her for too long. Without a word, she rolled over and positioned herself, on all fours, on the carpet in front of him. Every muscle felt tense as she waited for him to remove his jeans and kneel behind her. Her arms ached, her thighs shook as she waited, her breath rapid and too shallow, making her feel dizzy and lightheaded.

'Do you do this to yourself?' he asked suddenly, fingering her naked labia.

At the delicate caress, Ariane felt a rush of moisture well at the lip of her vagina. She sighed as she felt it overflow, bathing her parted labia. Brad rubbed in the heavy, honeyed secretions, entering her with two fingers and stretching her passage wide with a scissoring movement.

'You're tight,' he told her, his words inflaming her still further, 'and hot. So wet and hot and tight . . . open wider for me.'

Ariane slid her knees further apart on the carpet, feeling his warm breath brush the tender membranes of her open sex as he bent his head to lap at the juices running from her. His fingers strayed along the crease between her buttocks, dabbling at the resistant sphincter of her anus as he speared her with his tongue.

'Oh God – just do it!' she moaned, desperate for the teasing to stop and the fucking to begin.

Brad needed no further prompting. Ariane felt the head of his cock slide along the moist cleft of her sex, searching for the entrance to her body. He held her steady with a hand on each hip, then he pushed into her, burying himself in her with one swift, sure thrust.

'Oh!' she moaned, wriggling her hips and pressing back onto him further, desperate to deepen the penetration.

Sensing her need, Brad pushed harder, until his cockhead nudged the entrance to her womb, causing a shaft of pure, delicious pain to slice through her. It was a momentary discomfort, but it was enough to remind Ariane of Conrad. It could be his cock ramming into her from behind, his hands reaching beneath her to pull at her nipples until they burned and throbbed.

Ariane felt a fine film of perspiration break out on her skin as she rocked in time with every thrust. There was no finesse now, barely even any rapport between them. There was nothing except the instinct to mate like rutting animals, panting and grunting as they moved together towards climax.

'Harder!' she cried, thrusting her hips back to bounce off his iron-hard belly.

'I'll give it to you hard,' he panted, reaching round to hold the palm of his hand against her mound, pressing her against him with each inward stroke.

Ariane thought she would pass out with the intensity of it. Each time his body slammed against hers, she imagined that it was Conrad whom she had driven to lose control, Conrad who was labouring over her back, his body on fire as it plunged, over and over into hers.

'Yes – oh, yes!' she cried out as she came, her vaginal muscles convulsing around Brad's marauding cock, milking him to the point of no return.

'Uh . . . oh . . . sweet Jesus . . .' he muttered as his semen pumped along his shaft and burst out of him, into her body.

They collapsed together on the floor, a tangled mess of arms and legs, hot and sweaty and smeared with their combined emissions. Ariane felt as though her heart rate would never return to normal. Even her eyeballs ached.

As soon as he had caught his breath, Brad pulled out of her. Ariane sat up and watched him as he pulled on his clothes. He looked hot and dishevelled and he couldn't quite seem to meet her eye.

'You can stay for a drink, if you like,' she told him, amused rather than offended by his haste.

Brad glanced at her, and she realised that he wasn't confident of his ability to deliver a repeat performance if she should demand it.

'I have to get back to work.'

'Pity,' she said, mocking him.

Brad flushed, then, to her relief, he grinned.

'Sorry, but I really do have to go. It was great, though – thanks.'

'Thank *you*,' Ariane responded with a smile. 'You don't know how much I needed that!'

Dressed now, Brad looked at her quizzically.

'You're something else,' he said cryptically.

Ariane laughed. 'I know.'

She stood up and walked, naked, with him to the door.

'Goodbye.'

'Right. 'Bye.'

He half smiled at her, then, shaking his head, he walked through the door that she was holding open for him. With one last, lingering glance over his shoulder as he waited for the lift doors to open, he raised his hand and was gone. Ariane closed the door quietly behind him, feeling happy and satisfied, sure that she had found the key to her restlessness. It wasn't one-handed sex that she needed, but real, one-to-one fucking. And the next time she saw Conrad she was going to do her utmost to make him give her exactly what she needed.

Jon lay back in the huge, oval bath in Melissa's apartment and closed his eyes. He felt relaxed, replete in a way he couldn't ever remember feeling before. The water was hot and deep, filled with millions of fragrant bubbles which hissed gently in the silence.

There was a disturbance in the water and he opened his eyes to watch Melissa climb in. Catching a glimpse of her smooth, pink quim as she parted her legs, he felt his cock stir lazily, not so much with intention as with remembered pleasure. Once he had breached her defences it had been simple to persuade her that, since she had already sinned against Conrad, she might just as well submit totally to him while he was here.

He smiled at her now, watching as she piled her long, dark hair on top of her head and secured it with three strategically placed hair pins. Then she too sank into the water and her delectable body disappeared beneath the bubbles.

'Let me do that,' he said as she picked up an overly large bath sponge and poured a generous amount of liquid soap onto it.

'By all means!'

She handed him the sponge and Jon knelt up in the water and began to soap her neck and shoulders. Her skin was smooth and pink, velvety soft to the touch.

'You have lovely skin,' he told her, taking his time as he soaped her.

'Thank you. Will you remember me when you go back to England?'

The question, unexpected as it was, took him aback. Until now he had chosen not to think about leaving, he simply couldn't get enough of Melissa and the dark, erotic delights to which she had introduced him.

'Of course. Why don't you come with me?' he asked her impulsively.

She laughed softly, kneeling up in the water so that he could soap her breasts.

'Wouldn't Ariane object?'

Jon felt a pang of sadness, as he always did when he thought of Ariane recently.

'I don't see how things can continue between me and Ariane,' he admitted, putting his fears into words for the first time.

Turning her head, Melissa pressed her lips against the inside of his wrist.

'Have faith, Jon – what makes you think that Ariane won't have changed, too?'

Jon made a small, impatient gesture.

'Because she's not had the same experiences as me. I never realised how incomplete I felt until I met you.'

'But I'm not yours, Jon,' Melissa said gently. 'Ariane is your woman, just as I am Conrad's. I'm only on loan to you – just as Ariane is on loan to Conrad.'

Jon's hand slowed, then stilled as he began to realise what she was saying.

'What do you mean?' he asked.

Melissa looked up at him and smiled sympathetically.

'Do you think Conrad has been idle while you were away?'

'Are you trying to tell me he's been having an affair with my fiancée?'

'Not an affair, exactly. All I'm saying, Jon, is that from what Conrad tells me, you and Ariane might well be more compatible than you imagine.'

'I don't believe that Ariane would be unfaithful,' he said bluntly.

'Did you think you could be?'

'That's different.'

'Oh? How?'

Jon shrugged, aware that he sounded like a dinosaur.

'Ours is no ordinary affair. You've helped me discover my true self, Melissa, and that's no exaggeration. I've never known anything like this.'

'Then maybe Ariane has felt the same way? Go home with an open mind or you could miss so much.'

Jon didn't want to think about the possibility of Ariane sleeping with Conrad, discovering more about herself than she had known with him. Determined to change the subject, he squeezed water from the sponge over Melissa's face and neck. He watched the soapy water trickle across the surface of her skin and his cock rose to full hardness.

'I'm not going home for a while yet,' he said, his voice unnaturally husky. 'Lie back and let me wank over your beautiful skin.'

As always when he told her exactly what he intended to do, Melissa's face took on a dreamy, slightly unfocused look and she obeyed him at once. Looking up at him through wide, dark eyes, she parted her lips and allowed the tip of her tongue to slide along soft, pink skin. Standing over her, Jon took his penis in his hand and began to masturbate, using the sight of her naked body, just discernible beneath the thinning bubbles, as a visual spur.

Holding her eye, he imagined it was Ariane looking up at him with such exquisite submission and the speed of his orgasm took him by surprise. The ejaculate sprayed her breasts and the water surrounding her like a shower, exhausting him.

'Come here,' he said, sinking back into the water.

Melissa slid her body alongside his and kissed him, her warm, wet tongue searching his mouth. He held her close and knew, in that moment, that she was right -- he did still love Ariane. But his lust was reserved for Melissa. If only Ariane *was* the woman now lying in his arms in the rapidly cooling bath water, he would be the happiest man alive.

# *Eight*

'Your pleasure belongs to me. *You* belong to me.'

Ariane stared at Conrad, half fearful, half thrilled at his fury. She hadn't expected him tonight and her heart felt as though it had lodged in her throat when she had opened the door to find him standing there.

The first thing he did as she closed the door behind him was to lift her skirt. She hadn't replaced the leather strap after Brad had left a mere hour before, and he had guessed what she had been doing at once. As she had known he would, he knew that she had been masturbating while he had been away. Did he know how often, or for how long?

Ariane flinched away from the expression in his eyes as he looked at her. Now he was telling her exactly where she stood, and her stomach trembled in anticipation of his wrath.

'I know, Conrad. It was only because I was missing you so much – oh!'

She gasped as, without warning, he curled his fingers into the moist crevices of her vulva and pulled her towards him.

'I should have bound you tighter so that frigging yourself would have caused you pain.'

'Oh no!'

'You've not been doing it alone, though, have you my Angel?' he said silkily.

Ariane felt herself flush, giving herself away even as she shook her head.

'No, I mean, yes, I—'

Conrad lifted the fingers that had been inside her to her face and passed them beneath her nose. She could smell her own secretions on his fingers, mixed with the unmistakable odour of semen.

'Were you so desperate, Angel?' he crooned, pressing his fingers against her lips so that she could suck them clean.

Ariane screwed up her face in anguish as she licked and sucked at his skin. He began to stroke her with his other hand, his fingers slipping against her skin.

'Who was it?'

It did not cross her mind to refuse to tell him, she knew he would coax the information from her in the end.

'A taxi driver,' she replied, wincing at the look of amusement in his eyes.

'*A cab driver*? Was he good, Angel?'

She nodded.

'Young and strong?'

'Yes.'

'How did he take you, Angel?' He began to stroke her clitoris, moving the small hood of skin back and forth over the sensitive tip until she found it difficult to breathe.

'He . . . he took me from behind,' she whispered.

'Like a dog, Angel? A bitch on heat?'

'Yes.' Her voice broke on a sob and he began to strum her oversensitised flesh. Her legs felt weak and her heart beat an erratic tattoo in her chest.

'Please, Conrad – I can't bear it!' she pleaded.

'Oh, but you must!' he murmured, clearly aroused by her confession. 'Did you like it, Angel – did he fuck you long and hard?'

'Yes . . . oh . . .'

She could feel a climax building, knew that it could sweep over her at any second, before he had given her permission to come.

'The shame of it, Angel – debasing yourself with a stranger. Wasn't it good?'

'Yes! Yes it was. I imagined it was you . . .'

'Don't come, Angel,' he warned her, circling her clitoris with his fingertip more and more slowly until she felt the climax that had been building begin to ebb away.

She moaned, closing her eyes in momentary anguish.

'Oh, please!' she begged him, past caring how she compromised her pride.

'No,' he whispered, moving his hand away completely.

His face was inches from hers, his lips almost brushing her mouth as he spoke. She clung to him, murmuring incoherently into the shoulder of his jacket as she calmed herself.

Opening her eyes, Ariane saw that his had darkened to two deep, dark pools of desire. She knew better by now than to ask him to make love to her, but she wanted it, more than anything, she wanted it.

Conrad's expression changed as he read hers and his lips touched the corner of her mouth in a small, almost conciliatory kiss.

'You only did it for the pleasure of the punishment that you knew would follow,' he said.

Ariane did not answer, merely swaying slightly towards him,

wanting to feel the heat of him close to her. He smiled properly then.

'Let's go out to dinner,' he said unexpectedly. 'We can eat while I decide the best way to discipline you.'

Ariane almost groaned aloud as he moved away from her, but his words curled around her senses, keeping her on the boil. Excitement churned through her as she went to change. What would he do? How would he punish a transgression as serious as the one she had perpetrated that afternoon?

She dressed in a simple, black jersey cocktail dress which skimmed her figure rather than hugging it, hinting at its shape. The skirt was full around her calves and swirled as she walked, making her feel ultra feminine. Smoothing sheer black hold-ups on her legs, she decided to go without panties, in the hope that Conrad might have more pleasures in store for her while they were out.

He'd never taken her out in public before and she found she was strangely excited, rather like a teenager on a first date. Slipping her feet in high heeled black sandals, she fixed her face and brushed her hair before going out to meet him.

He was on the telephone, though his eyes caressed her approvingly as he finished his conversation.

'I've ordered a cab,' he told her, his lips twitching with amusement as he saw the rush of colour to her face. 'Let's hope it isn't *your* driver.'

'Where are we going?' she asked him, not really caring at all.

'A small club I found while I was away.'

He would not be drawn any further and Ariane had to be content with that.

In the taxi, Ariane felt his eyes on her more than once and her skin prickled with a heightened awareness of him. Knowing that his attention was fully on her, planning their evening, deciding how he would pleasure her, gave her a deep, primitive thrill which she knew she never wanted to lose.

The club he had spoken of was located along a dark side road just out of town. Large, dilapidated Edwardian terraces marched the length of the street on either side of the road, giving the area a run down feel that made her feel uneasy, out of place.

As Conrad paid the driver, Ariane looked around, apprehensively. The street was badly lit, the club advertised by a single, broken neon sign which swung creakily in the light wind. It didn't look like the sort of place to which she would normally go, and she felt uncomfortable as Conrad opened the door for her.

Inside, they walked down a dingy staircase to what would once have been the kitchens. Now the dividing walls had been removed and it was decorated in red with streaks of blue here and there, more appropriate to a warehouse than a club, The tables were arranged around a small, raised dais, lit by a single spotlight. There was a small dance floor to one side where a couple were moving slowly to the music pounding from the jukebox, apparently oblivious to the beat, draped over each other as if each needed the other's support to remain upright. The girl had her eyes closed, as if the weight of the thick, dark make-up smeared round them was too much for her eyelids to bear.

By the bar that ran the length of one wall, several scantily dressed women were sitting on bar stools. As one, they all looked up hopefully as Ariane and Conrad walked in, losing interest as soon as they saw there was no trade to be had. A sweet, sickly odour hung in a pall about the place, mixing with the fug of cigarette smoke that caught at the back of Ariane's throat.

'You've brought me to a strip joint?' she said, incredulously.

Conrad did not answer, he merely led her to one of the tables, near to the dais.

'I can't believe you've brought me here!' she hissed as he pulled out her chair.

'Sit down,' he said, his voice low, but compelling. 'Watch and learn.'

A waitress in a short dress and seamed stockings came to take their order. Conrad asked for champagne and strawberries, nothing else. The waitress batted her false eyelashes at him and he smiled at her as if she was the most exquisite woman in the room.

'Have a drink yourself,' he said, the picture of urbane charm, and the woman fluttered coyly, leaning over him to clear the table of the empty glasses that had been left there. Her breasts, almost spilling over the top of her uniform, brushed against his face. Conrad planted a small kiss on the downward sweep of one jiggling globe and smiled at her as she straightened. The waitress gave him one last, longing look over her shoulder as she walked away, swaying her hips provocatively.

'Why did you do that?' Ariane asked him furiously when, at last, they were alone again.

'Do what?'

'Flirt like that with the waitress. It was humiliating!'

Conrad regarded her intently from across the table. After a few minutes of this scrutiny, Ariane shifted uncomfortably in her chair, waiting for his reaction.

'I don't recall asking you your opinion,' he said coldly.

'What?' She laughed.

Conrad stared unblinkingly back at her and Ariane felt her mouth dry as she realised he was serious.

She turned her head as a blast of sound made her jump. All eyes swivelled to the raised platform as, appearing from nowhere, it seemed, two women took up position. The first was tall and blonde with wild, permed hair, the second shorter with a reddish brown crop which showed off her elfin features. Both were dressed in high heeled boots and spangled bikinis trimmed with fringes which shook as they danced.

Ariane felt supremely uncomfortable. Glancing around her, she saw the excited faces of the clientele, heard the crude remarks and catcalls, smelt the overwhelming odours of cigarettes, and sweat and sexual tension, and knew she was way out of her depth.

'Conrad . . .'

'Ssh. Watch.'

In spite of herself, Ariane watched. The two women were facing each other, shimmying and shaking for all they were worth. The champagne arrived and Ariane lifted her filled glass to her lips without consciously realising what she was doing. The bubbles stung her nose and she coughed, earning herself a look of reproof from Conrad.

The tension in the room rose a notch as the blonde woman reached for her partner and took off her bra. The redhead had small, high breasts topped by cherry red nipples which glistened under the harsh spotlight. Removing her own top, the blonde shook her big breasts until they swayed, the large, pink areolae staying soft and wide, like a delicate smudge of paint in the centre of each breast.

Moving together, the two women kissed, their arms coming about each other so that their bodies were pressed close together. The audience went wild, cheering them on as their tongues met and parried and their breasts flattened together.

Ariane had never seen two women kissing before, and, watching, she was appalled and fascinated in equal measure. The women on the stage, though there was no doubt that they performed like professionals, seemed to be oblivious to the presence of their audience. There was a sensuality about the way they were caressing each other that was far from false. Ariane found herself wondering about them. Were they lovers off stage as well as on?

Glancing at Conrad, she saw that he was watching her, watching them. His lips curved upwards slightly in the curious half smile she had come to know, and he passed her the bowl of fresh, hulled strawberries. Ariane picked one and dipped it, first into a bowl of sugar, then into the cream. Without fully realising what she was doing, she pressed the fruit between her teeth, holding his eye.

'More,' he mouthed as the sharp flesh of the strawberry slipped down her throat, eased by the thick, cold cream.

Ariane obliged, eating another of the strawberries, sweet and overripe, licking her fingers clean, one by one. On the stage, the women were now naked, kneeling on the floor as their hands roamed each other's bodies. As Ariane watched, they manoeuvred themselves gracefully into a classic sixty-nine and set to work with lips and tongues.

'Have you ever wondered what it would be like to lick out another woman?'

Conrad's voice was low in her ear and she realised that he had moved his chair to her side of the table. She had been so absorbed in the action on the stage that she hadn't noticed him move.

'No!' she said quickly now. 'I've never been curious about doing it with another woman.'

'Are you sure?'

Conrad seemed amused by her vehemence and he raked her cheek with tiny, breathy kisses, making her shiver.

'Never,' she repeated emphatically.

'Liar!'

Ariane glanced at him, shocked.

'I have not!' she said indignantly. Conrad ignored her.

'Imagine,' he whispered in her ear, 'imagine the feel of soft, pliable flesh pressing against yours. Sweet, womanly smells. A protracted, feminine sigh in response to your caress. Wouldn't you like that, Angel?'

'No!' she whispered, her tone unconvincing even to her own ears.

'Oh, I think you would!'

His voice was invidious, trickling over her senses like warm honey, coaxing a response from her. His hand was warm as he rested it on her thigh, describing small, sensitive circles on the skin, edging ever closer to the centre of her. Ariane was aware that her sex had swollen and was slick with moisture. In a moment his fingers would find that warm, dew-soaked core of her and he would know beyond a doubt that she was lying.

'*I'd* like to see you with another girl,' he was saying now, his voice husky with desire. 'Oh, yes, I can just see you now, burying your face in her sweet cunt, lapping at her juices . . .'

Ariane stared at the blonde woman as she licked and sucked at the other girl's sex and imagined herself in her place.

'Can you taste her, Angel? Can you feel that sweet honey on your tongue?'

She moaned softly in response, closing her eyes and swallowing hard as his fingers brushed against her swollen labia.

'Ah, yes, I know you can! Watch, Angel – open your legs.'

Under the table, Ariane slid her feet apart to give him access to her heated flesh. The women on the stage were moaning and writhing now, close to climax and her clitoris throbbed empathetically.

'That's it – wider . . . good girl, Angel . . . let it come . . . when they come, I want you to come, too. Open your mouth.'

Ariane obeyed him without taking her eyes from the tableau in front of her. Conrad tipped a little champagne onto her tongue and she swallowed obediently, without thought. She felt so hot, so unbearably aroused, she almost felt she could be on the stage with them. The redhead's legs were wrapped now around the blonde's neck and her hips bucked as she crested.

Imagining how it would feel to have her tongue pressed close to another woman's spasming clitoris, Ariane bore down, climaxing with a shudder and a groan, swiftly muffled by Conrad's mouth descending on hers.

He kissed her until the tremors died away, then he pulled back, scanning her face with eyes that were dark and unreadable.

'Finish the strawberries,' he said, 'I have to make a call.'

Ariane felt dazed as he left her. She was disoriented to find that the show was over, the women had disappeared. Feeling as if she was being watched, she turned her head to find that the man on the table to her left was staring intently at her. He was middle-aged and unkempt, with thick, rubbery lips which glistened moistly in the dim lighting. As she caught his eye, he gave her a leering, knowing look and she quickly looked away, appalled that he had witnessed her shame.

Where was Conrad? Ariane looked around her frantically, afraid that he might have left her there, alone. Spotting him making his way back to the table, she relaxed, confident that he would keep her from harm.

'Time to go,' he told her, holding out his hand.

Ariane took it gratefully and stood up, eager now to leave.

He took her back to his hotel suite. Stopping only to take her coat, he led her by the hand into the living room and offered her a seat on the sofa. There were three lamps placed around the room, and he switched them all on, leaving the curtains tied back so that the luminescent white glow of the moon spilled across the carpet. Crouching in front of her, his expression was oddly intent. He seemed to be full of adrenalin, as if his entire body vibrated silently with barely controlled desire.

Ariane was aroused by this evidence that he was attracted to her – it made her feel powerful, feminine in the most basic of ways. Yet still she waited warily for him to reveal his intentions towards her, knowing that the night ahead would be nothing if not inventive. Painful, probably, but certainly never dull. She shivered.

'Are you cold, Angel?' he asked her, picking up one of her hands and chafing it between his.

'No.' She smiled, liking the way his eyes were glowing a deep, leonine gold in the semi-darkness.

Feeling bold, she reached out to trace the line of his jaw with her fingertips. His skin was roughened slightly by the defiant stubble pushing through his pores. He was clearly a man who had to shave twice daily, but Ariane was glad he hadn't shaved before they went out. Somehow the thought of his strong chin rasping gently over her bare skin made her inner muscles clench with excitement.

Holding her eye, Conrad caught the tip of her forefinger between his lips and sucked it into his mouth. Ariane watched, fascinated, as his cheeks hollowed and his tongue circled her finger. Slowly, he drew his head back, then, just as he reached the tip of her finger, he bit down on the soft pad, hard enough to make her pull away sharply.

Shaking her throbbing finger, she glared at him.

'That hurt!' she complained, disappointed that, as always, he had turned pleasure into pain.

His smile was almost affectionate.

'Are you hungry?' he asked her.

'A little,' she admitted, surprised at the question.

'I'll feed you,' he said, leaping to his feet and striding over to the telephone.

Ariane watched him as he spoke into the receiver. She loved the way his throat muscles rippled as he spoke, adored the strong, angular shape of his face. Longing to touch him, to slide her body over his, she found herself leaning towards him, earning herself a raised eyebrow. Forcing herself back in her seat, Ariane regained her self-control, earning herself an approving glance.

God, what had he done to her? She felt as though she lived for his approval, a smile, a gentle touch from him worth any discomfort or humiliation. He trained her to respond rather as he might train a dog – sit – good girl – reward . . .

He ordered oysters and wine from room service before replacing the receiver. Turning all his attention onto Ariane, he smiled slowly.

'Will you let me blindfold you?' he asked.

Ariane gazed at him in surprise.

'Blindfold me?' she echoed faintly.

The request was unexpected, the sudden leap of excitement the words invoked, inexplicable to her. The idea of being totally at his mercy, unable to see what he was doing, frightened as much as thrilled her. Conrad regarded her steadily, as if savouring her apprehension.

'Trust me,' he said. 'You know I know what you need.'

His choice of words made her shiver, and a dull pulse began to beat between her thighs.

'Yes,' she whispered.

He had an eye mask made of soft black leather, lined with red silk. Ariane held her breath as he positioned it over the bridge of her nose, smoothing it lovingly over her face until there was not so much as a chink of light creeping in around the edges.

'All right?' he whispered, his fingertips tracing the contours of her face with a light, loving touch.

Ariane swallowed. She felt very isolated, deprived of her sight, vulnerable in a way she had never experienced before. She clutched ineffectually at Conrad's sleeve as he moved away from her, feeling the fabric slip out of her grasp as he stood up.

'Don't leave me!' she said, despising the note of panic she could hear in her own voice.

'I won't leave you, Angel,' he promised.

She jumped as she heard a sharp rap on the door. Straining her ears, she heard Conrad walk across the room, then open it.

'Ah – room service!' he heard him say. 'Come in. Put the tray on the coffee table, please.'

Every muscle in Ariane's body tensed as she sensed the waiter walk across the room and come towards her. What would he think when he saw her wearing the blindfold? Visions of the suite being stormed by the local constabulary, bent on rescuing her, flitted through her mind and she had to suppress the urge to giggle.

She sensed the waiter's steps falter as he caught sight of her and heard his sharp intake of breath, swiftly hidden.

'Don't mind my friend,' Conrad said. 'It's a little game we play. Like a party trick, you know, where you have to guess what you are eating? Isn't that right, Angel?'

'Yes,' she replied, imagining the waiter's uncertainty as he looked from her to Conrad and back again.

'Of course, sir,' she heard him say, stiffly. There was a rattle of crockery as he set the tray down on the coffee table as instructed. 'My wife and I play it all the time, sir.'

He left and as soon as he had closed the door after him, Ariane heard Conrad chuckle. It was the first time she had ever heard him laugh aloud and she cherished the sound, wanting to hear it again.

'Poor guy didn't know where to look,' he told her as he came back to her side. 'Maybe next time he comes we should have you properly displayed – give him something to really be shocked about. "*My wife and I play it all the time, sir*",' he mimicked the man's prim response so accurately that Ariane laughed. 'Do they, my ass!'

'Didn't he look like the kind of man to play, Conrad?'

'You think we're playing, Angel?'

'I . . . yes, I think we are,' she replied, knowing at once that she was talking herself into a corner.

She shivered as Conrad suddenly, unexpectedly, reached out to fondle her breast through the thin fabric of her dress. He stroked his thumb unhurriedly over her nipple, as if considering her response. Ariane felt her skin contract, her nipple drawing into a peak. Conrad pressed gently on the hard bead at the tip, not hard enough to hurt her, but firmly enough to make her gasp.

'This isn't a game, Angel. This is life. Your life, my life. Jon's life. I'm training you, Angel, giving you the knowledge by which you can keep your man.'

Ariane frowned.

'What do you mean?' she asked, her voice small.

'You'll see,' he said softly. 'Now – we have fresh oysters here. Open your mouth and I'll feed you some.'

Ariane tried to ignore the apprehension churning through her, opening her mouth obediently as Conrad touched her lips with the cool, hard shell. The oyster slipped into her mouth and down her throat so smoothly it felt as though it had been liquidised especially for her. Holding a glass to her lips, Conrad helped her to wash it down with crisp white wine, not content until she had drained the glass.

She felt a dribble run down her chin and tried to catch it with her tongue, in vain. Seeing it, Conrad bent his head and caught it on his, bringing it up to her lips and feeding it back to her, mixed with his saliva. They kissed, deeply. Conrad took time to probe and lick at the tender membranes inside her lips, his touch so gentle it started in Ariane a deep, unfulfilled yearning that she didn't understand. She wanted . . . she wasn't sure what it was she wanted, she could only be sure that it was unobtainable.

'Now,' he said after he had pulled away and repeated the procedure twice more, 'I have a little treat for you. Come through to the bedroom.'

Ariane stood up and swayed unsteadily. Three glasses of wine in quick succession had gone straight to her head, making her feel dizzy. Seeing this, Conrad put out his hand and guided her into his room.

As soon as she felt the smooth satin of the duvet against the backs of her legs, Ariane sat down gratefully. Behind the blindfold, it felt as though the room was spinning crazily and she longed to lie down and close her eyes . . .

'Stand up at once!' Conrad barked.

She obeyed with alacrity, stumbling slightly as she jumped to her feet.

'Did I tell you to sit?' he asked her wearily.

'No,' she admitted, 'but—'

'No "buts" – you either do as you are told or we stop right now. Is that what you want?'

Feeling the pulse which had been beating steadily between her thighs ever since they had arrived quicken, Ariane shook her head.

'Oh, no,' she said fervently.

'Good. Then you will wait for my instructions from now on?'

'Yes.'

'Take off your clothes.'

Ariane heard the springs of the bed dip as Conrad threw himself down on it and knew that he was watching her as she stripped. It was surprisingly difficult to undress blindfolded. First, she took off her shoes, allowing her stockinged feet to sink gratefully into the pile of the carpet. Lifting her skirt she rolled down her hold-ups, one by one.

'You have beautiful legs, Angel,' Conrad said, his voice low and caressing, encouraging her to continue.

Ariane raised her skirts slowly, anticipating the moment when he would see that she wasn't wearing anything else. His sharp intake of breath thrilled her. That small betrayal of his own arousal returned to her a modicum of power, a fleeting sensation of equality that spurred her on.

As she pulled the dress up, over her head, she stretched upwards, offering him a perfect view of her body, glorious in its nakedness. Though she could not see him, she could hear him breathing and knew that she *did* have power over him, that her acceptance, or rejection of his demands was the axis on which their relationship turned. His dominance was dependent on her willingness to submit.

The notion was a seductive one and, for the first time, Ariane accepted the role in which she had been cast without reservation.

Realising that by giving him dominion over her she had in fact made her own choices was liberating, freeing her to enjoy each experience to the full, without the guilt which had dogged her.

She stood, naked and exposed in front of him and waited for him to speak. He didn't. Instead, he moved so that he was sitting at the end of the bed, his knees spread so that they were either side of her closed thighs. Pulling her towards him, he pressed his lips against the womanly swell of her belly, dipping his tongue into her navel and licking a small, wet path up to the valley between her breasts.

Unable to see him, Ariane had no way of knowing what he intended to do next. She sighed as she felt his mouth close over one nipple as he fed her breast into his mouth. The sensations as he suckled at her breast were exquisite, travelling through to her womb and transmitting little messages of pleasure through to the slippery folds of skin between her thighs.

She felt hot and breathless as he began to suck harder, his teeth grazing the swollen flesh of her areola as the suckling became more fierce, until the sensations it created bordered on the painful.

'Conrad . . .' she said, her voice cracking as he bit, none too gently, on her nipple. 'You're hurting me,' she whispered, not altogether sure that she wanted him to stop.

He raised his head for an instant and she sensed that he smiled at her. Then, without replying, he turned his attention to her other breast, sucking hungrily on it, rolling the nipple on his tongue and scraping the sensitive skin with his teeth.

Little shards of pleasure-pain pierced her, reflected in the throbbing between her legs. If he touched her there, now, she knew that she would come. A kaleidoscope of colour was poised behind her eyelids, on the brink of spinning out of control the moment he pressed the small, shiny button that was the centre of her pleasure.

He didn't touch her, instead he suddenly put her from him and stood up.

'That's better,' he said, conversationally, as if he had just helped her to tidy her hair rather than ravage her breasts. 'You look like a wanton, ready for anything. I've brought something for you to wear – very pretty, it's a pity you can't see it. Perhaps later.'

Ariane cocked her head and listened as he walked across the room and opened the door to the wardrobe. She heard the sound of a suitcase opening and the faint rustle of tissue paper as something was unwrapped.

'What is it?' she asked him, trying unsuccessfully to mask her apprehension.

'It's a whore's costume – very becoming. Arms up.'

Ariane obeyed, despite her misgivings. What did he mean, a whore's costume? She felt the uncompromising chill of metal links as he passed something over her head and fastened a buckle at the back of her neck.

'Not too tight? Good. This is a neck collar, attached to which is the most exquisite body harness. This bit here passes between your breasts, to separate them . . .' he paused as he fastened a second buckle in the centre of her back, '. . . beautiful! The strap splits in two just below your navel, so it frames your mound, passing either side of your labia, like . . . so!'

Ariane gasped as the two halves of the strap were buckled round either thigh. In her mind's eye, she saw herself, blindfolded, strapped into a garment made purely for sex, designed to draw attention to the most intimate parts of her body. To her shame, the thought made her juices flow anew, filming the inside of her upper thighs with moisture.

Conrad noticed and bent to kiss her approvingly on the lips.

'You're a quick study, Angel – and so responsive! You're one of the best I've trained so far.'

Ariane felt a surge of jealousy at the implication that she was merely the latest in a long line of many, and she pouted, eliciting a low chuckle from Conrad.

'Now for the finishing touch,' he said softly.

Ariane waited, every muscle in her body held taut as she wondered what he would do next. She gasped as he grasped one tumescent nipple between his finger and thumb and tweaked it, pulling it away from her body. Bending his head to it, he sucked it into his mouth, elongating it sufficiently for him to be able to slip a cold, metal ring around it.

Behind the silk-lined blindfold, Ariane's eyes watered at the discomfort.

'It . . . it's too tight,' she complained bravely.

If she had expected any sympathy, or the slightest hint of mercy, she was disappointed.

'Good,' he replied shortly, 'a little pain will be good for you. Now, prepare the other one for its ring.'

Appalled at what he wanted her to do, Ariane fingered her unfettered nipple half-heartedly.

'Pathetic!' Conrad said, though he seemed more amused than annoyed. 'Do you want me to whip them?'

'No!' she said, alarmed at the idea.

'But I shall, my Angel, I shall.'

Something clicked in Ariane's chest, something dark and primitive. She moaned softly as Conrad sucked her nipple into prominence before imprisoning it with another ring. She brought her hands up to her breasts and covered them protectively. The metal rings were shockingly cold against her fingers, her tortured nipples pressing against the centre of her palms.

'I'm going to tie your hands behind you,' he told her, as casually as if he was informing her of his decision to order dinner.

Ariane knew better than to resist as he positioned her hands at the small of her back, wincing as the cold steel of the handcuffs he had produced touched against her skin. As soon as they had clicked into place, Conrad placed his hand on the nape of her neck and pressed gently, forcing her to bend from the waist.

'Be brave, my Angel,' he said, pressing his lips against her ear.

Ariane shook as she listened to him open the suitcase again and take something out. She sensed, rather than heard him approach her again.

'Relax,' he said softly, stroking her bent back and massaging her tense shoulders, soothing her. 'This is just something to warm you up a little. You've suffered far worse.'

Somehow the idea of being whipped on the breasts was far more alarming than presenting the more robust shape of her bottom for punishment. Ariane trembled anew as he made her wait, until she was almost on the verge of begging him to start, just so that it would soon be over.

He used something thin and whippy which, she was sure, could have caused her damage had he wielded it harshly. He didn't, but as it was, the first stroke, placed precisely on the underside of her breasts, took her breath away.

Ariane gritted her teeth, determined not to give way to the tears that were gathering behind the blindfold. Somehow, she knew that he would not be impressed by tears, that her fortitude was a tribute to him. Five strokes, he administered, no more than sharp taps, really, but causing five stinging stripes that left her panting, her entire body filmed with perspiration. With each stroke, her breasts quivered and shook, her nipples pulsing against the rings constraining them.

When he had finished, he helped her to stand upright, then he soothed her burning flesh with saliva, running his tongue along the lightly raised weals, both increasing the discomfort, and drawing out the pleasure creeping beneath the pain.

Ariane could not understand how joy and misery could be so closely connected, but pushed away any rational analysis. At that moment she didn't care *why*, she merely welcomed the fact that it was so. She was proud of her stoicism, glad that she had borne the punishment without a sound. She knew that she had been a credit to him. Perhaps he would show his appreciation of her fortitude with his cock – she had waited for so long.

'Poor love,' he murmured against her hair, before taking her into his arms and kissing her upturned face. 'Sweet Angel! You're to rest now – later I'll reward you for your courage.'

He led her over to the bed and, unfastening the handcuffs, he pressed her onto her back. The satin was cold against her heated skin and she shivered. Conrad lay down beside her and gathered her into his arms, offering her the warmth of his body. It was rare for him to allow her so close, and Ariane revelled in the sensation of his lean, lithe body pressing against hers, his clothes brushing erotically against her naked skin.

He said he would reward her – did that mean that he would make love to her at last? He knew her body like no one else, he had led her down the path of debauchery like an erotic Pied Piper, yet he had never attempted to fuck her. Ariane found herself hoping that this would be her reward.

She made a small moue of distress as he moved away from her and she felt a chill pass over her skin.

'I'm going to tie you to the bed now, Angel, and let you rest.

You're going to need all your stamina for later.'

Ariane lay, acquiescent as a rag doll as he wrapped silk scarves around her wrists and ankles and tied her, spread-eagle fashion, to the bed. She gasped as, unexpectedly, he bent his head and placed a small kiss on the very tip of her exposed clitoris before moving away from her. The tiny bundle of nerve endings tingled where his lips had touched and Ariane knew that the small gesture would stay with her while she waited, keeping her on the verge of orgasm, but without the means to satisfy her craving. Such sweet torture!

A sheet fluttered across her naked body and Conrad bent to kiss her, lingeringly, on the lips. She loved the taste of his mouth, would have been happy to lie in this position for hours while he kissed her. He, too, seemed reluctant to stop. After he pulled back, Ariane sensed that he watched her.

'I'll leave you for a while now, Angel,' he said.

'What about the blindfold?' she asked him, panicking at the idea of being left alone in her own, personal darkness.

He soothed her by stroking her hair and caressing the soft leather of the blindfold where it moulded the bridge of her nose and her cheekbones, with his fingertips.

'Just close your eyes, Angel – think about later. I'll be back.'

He crossed the room and closed the door quietly behind him, leaving her alone.

'Conrad?' she whispered uncertainly.

There was no answer, just the silence pounding in her ears.

# Nine

Jon lay back on the grass beside Melissa, replete after the huge picnic she had brought to work with her. Bagels and soft cheese, strawberries, grapes and cherries, sticky chocolate pie, all washed down with cold beer. Now he felt drowsy and satisfied, totally disinclined to move, let alone head back towards the office as he ought to.

'I thought Central Park was supposed to be a no-go area,' he said sleepily, gazing up at peerless blue sky. 'I never dreamt it would be so beautiful.'

'So long as you're sensible it's okay,' Melissa said, raising herself up on one elbow and looking at him. 'I wouldn't recommend you stroll through here on your own at night, for example.'

Jon looked around him at the children dancing excitedly around their mothers' and nannies' feet, at the mixture of teenagers and smart city suits rollerblading along the pathways, all enjoying the glorious sunshine, and he found it hard to believe that such a transformation could take place after dark.

Melissa leaned over him, blocking out the sun. Her features were in shadow, but he sensed that her expression was melancholy. He felt a rush of tenderness towards her and realised that he had become very fond of her over the past few weeks. Her long, dark hair fell forward and brushed his face and Jon reached up to tuck it over her shoulder.

'What is it?' he asked her softly.

She shook her head, giving a small, self-deprecating laugh.

'It's been . . . good to be with you,' she said, her voice low and filled with regret.

Jon sat up, alarmed.

'I don't go back until a week on Saturday. It sounds as if you're telling me it's over,' he said, scanning her face for a clue to her thoughts.

Melissa kept her eyes lowered.

'Conrad phoned today. He tells me you'll be going home a few days earlier so that you can work together to synchronise operations.'

'No one's told me this,' he said indignantly.

She looked up then, and smiled at him.

'The message will probably be on your desk when we get back. There is some good news, though.'

'Oh?'

'Conrad wants me to travel with you. I'll stay to meet Ariane, then I'll travel back with Conrad when he comes home. What do you think?'

Jon stared at her, pulled apart by conflicting emotions. On the one hand he wanted to get home, to see Ariane and find out if there was any way for them to move forward together. On the other, he wanted to stay here, suspended in time, with Melissa as his ever-willing consort.

'Why would you want to meet Ariane?' he asked her after a few moments, homing in on the most puzzling aspect of her announcement.

Melissa had a mischievous glint in her eye that Jon did not quite trust.

'You've told me so much about her, I have a feeling that we'd get on well.'

'I don't think you would,' he countered bluntly.

Melissa shrugged, not wanting to argue.

'Whatever. *You* must be looking forward to seeing her.'

'Must I?' he muttered, lying down again and throwing one arm across his eyes to shield them from the glare of the sun.

'Yes.' She bent to kiss him softly on the lips. 'Have faith, darling – everything will turn out just fine.'

'I don't see how it can.' Jon sighed heavily. 'There's no going back for me now, you've opened my eyes to things I never dreamed existed.'

'Why not introduce Ariane to your new experiences?'

Jon frowned, shocked at the idea.

'I could never do the things I do with you with Ariane. She'd be horrified!'

Melissa trailed her long fingers over his lips thoughtfully.

'How can you be so sure? Didn't you ever feel like chastising Ariane while you were in bed together?'

Jon felt his face flood with warm colour.

'Of course not,' he lied vehemently.

Melissa smiled and he knew she didn't believe him.

'Tell me how it is between you and Ariane,' she said quietly.

He could have told her to mind her own business, but somehow he found he wanted to talk. Besides, soon he and Melissa would part and they were unlikely to meet again. What harm could it possibly do to talk to her about his deepest, darkest thoughts?

'Ariane is . . . delicate,' he began, seeing again in his mind's eye his fiancée's pale skin, soft blonde hair and trusting blue eyes. 'Sometimes, when we make love, I feel as if she could break in half in my arms . . . why are you looking at me like that?'

'You sound as if she's a porcelain doll, not a living, breathing woman!'

'You don't understand. I love Ariane, I would never want to hurt her.'

'Only bring her pleasure?'

'Yes.'

'Haven't you learned yet how much pleasure can be had through the controlled application of pain?'

'It's different with you,' he insisted stubbornly.

Smiling, Melissa lay down beside him, resting her head on her hand. Gazing across the park, her eyes took on a faraway expression, telling him that she had gone to a place inside herself where he could not follow. He felt the frustration zinging through his veins and had to make an effort to keep his impatience in check. She'd come back to him, when she was ready.

'I know you find this hard to believe,' she said after a few minutes, 'but Conrad loves me. Our relationship began as a conventional one, not unlike yours with Ariane. When he made love to me he used to handle me as if he was afraid that I would break.' She laughed softly. 'It took me months to gather the courage to tell him how I longed for him to take me savagely, to ravish me without warning, to use my body as if it were a thing made purely for his pleasure.'

Melissa flung herself onto her back on the grass, throwing out her arms in theatrical abandonment, her face wreathed in smiles. Rolling onto his stomach, Jon watched her, absorbing every detail of her face, committing it to memory. She seemed to glow, with health and happiness and self-assurance. The contrast between this together, confident young woman and the supplicant she liked to play behind the bedroom door was so marked that Jon became hard just thinking about it. He doubted he could ever tire of contemplating the dichotomy.

'What did he say when you finally told him?' he asked her curiously.

Melissa's eyes sparkled at him as she answered.

'He didn't *say* anything. He told me it was unladylike to admit such things. At first, I laughed – I thought he was kidding me. Then I realised he wasn't, that he really was angry, and I got a funny feeling, right here.' Pressing her hand flat against the top of her pubis, she closed her eyes for a moment, remembering.

'Go on,' Jon prompted, impatient to hear what had happened.

Opening her eyes, Melissa continued, her voice lower, redolent of remembered passion.

'He said he would have to punish me, that he was going to give me a good spanking. I wasn't sure whether to slap his face, or walk out, or tell him not be so ridiculous.'

'What *did* you do?'

'He didn't give me the chance to do anything. We were in the library at his parents' house, an old-fashioned room with a big, leather swivel chair by the French windows. Conrad grabbed me by the arm and, sitting down in the chair, he pulled me over his knee. I was wearing cotton pants and a cropped T-shirt, showing off my tan. Conrad yanked my pants down to my knees, panties and all.'

'And you let him?'

'I fought him like a hellcat – he had the scars where I raked my fingernails across his face for over a month!' she laughed at the memory, then her eyes misted over as she recalled what happened next. 'Conrad was so mad, he really meant it by the time he started to spank me. I yelled and hollered, but there was no-one in the house but us, no-one to hear.'

'Did it hurt?' Jon could just imagine her lying over Conrad's lap, trousers and underwear round her ankles, her pert little bottom exposed to the flat of his hand.

'Hell, yes – of course it hurt! At first, that was all I could think. I kept yelling, "It hurts! It hurts!" but the more I hollered, the harder and faster he spanked me. Then a funny thing happened.'

'What was that?'

'I gradually realised that I was getting horny, that there was a kind of throbbing ache between my legs that grew stronger every time his hand cracked across my bottom. I could feel that Conrad had an erection, and the idea of his being turned on by it, too, made me wetter, and hotter.'

'What did he do?'

'He stopped and began to rub it better. His hand must have been stinging almost as much as my bottom, but he carried on stroking me, letting his fingers dip into my cleft and smearing my juices over my burning skin. Before too long, I was bucking my hips, trying to rub my clit against his thigh, desperate to relieve the ache that was building up inside me. I felt like I would explode, I was so ready to come.'

Jon ran his fingers down her hair, lifting up a hank of it and rubbing it over his face. It still smelled of the coconut shampoo with which he had washed it the night before and he inhaled deeply.

'And did you come, baby?' he murmured.

'Conrad lifted me up and ordered me to take off my pants. I'll tell you, the sound of his voice, the way he spoke to me, I almost came there and then. I couldn't do it fast enough! While I was doing that, he was unfastening his trousers and getting out his prick. It was huge, bigger than I'd ever seen it before. I couldn't take my eyes off it as I waited for him to tell me what he wanted me to do.'

'Waiting?'

'Yes. I just knew that he had to be the one to decide. I wanted him to call the shots.'

'What *did* he decide?'

'He told me to climb onto his lap and feed his prick into me. Then he made me lean back, just far enough so that the penetration hurt a little. I had to do all the work, he just sat there with an odd look on his face, watching me. I moved up and down on his prick, watching it appear and disappear, burying itself deeper and deeper inside me with each thrust. Conrad waited until he was just about to come, then he started to rub my clit. We came together, so hard and so long that I thought I was going to pass out.'

'Did you?'

'No. But that was the start of something special, something I wouldn't have missed for all the world.'

Jon gazed at her and frowned.

'Yet now he sends you messages to fuck other men? How come?'

Melissa laughed at his confusion.

'Well, you see, at first I used to go out of my way to annoy him, to make life difficult, just so that I could provoke him into spanking me. It got so that day to day life was hell, we only stayed together for the sex. Gradually, though, we evolved a way of keeping it contained, a way that we could work and live together in harmony and still have great sex whenever we wanted.'

Jon ran his fingertip from her outstretched hand to her armpit, tracing a ticklish line along the inside of her arm. Her skin was soft and silky, still faintly perfumed with the expensive body lotion he had massaged into her the night before.

'Are you trying to say that Ariane might be yearning to tumble down off the pedestal I've put her on?'

'Ah, so you do admit you've put her on a pedestal!'

Jon grimaced, kissing the tender place inside the crook of her elbow.

'Maybe a little,' he admitted.

'Would you like to kiss her feet of clay?' Melissa asked, smiling at him.

A brief, shocking image of Ariane bent over his knee while he warmed her bottom flashed through Jon's mind. He had an instant erection and Melissa chuckled, covering it with her hand.

'You see?' she said, in a way that made him think she could read his mind. 'The penis never lies!'

Jon lay back, holding his hand over hers when she went to remove it.

'Just for that,' he said, watching her lazily through half closed eyes, 'I expect some recompense.'

'Here?' she said, glancing around her nervously.

'Uh-huh. Hand and mouth.'

Melissa gazed at him for a moment, her expression unreadable. Her long fingers kneaded him through his trousers, cupping his balls and trickling along his shaft teasingly.

'I think you'd be very happy with Ariane, now,' she told him with conviction.

'What makes you so sure?'

'You'll see,' she said, cryptically.

'You act as if you know something I don't,' he said, frustration reverberating through every word. 'You don't know Ariane at all, so why do you think she'll welcome me back so readily?'

Melissa would not be drawn. Using her hair as a curtain to

shield her face, she began to caress him with her mouth through the thin fabric of his suit trousers. Jon wanted to press her, to make her explain herself, but she was drawing his zip down with her teeth and the touch of her soft, plump lips against the bare skin of his belly was enough to drive everything else out of his mind.

He lay back and tried to behave in nonchalant fashion as Melissa lifted his penis through his flies and drew the tip into the heated cavern of her mouth. All around them, life continued in its usual pattern. Though there was no one in their immediate vicinity, they were close enough to a path for Jon to watch anxiously for anyone walking past in case they glanced across and saw them.

With her back to the path, he guessed that anyone seeing Melissa bent over him might assume she had merely draped herself over him as lovers do, that maybe she had a magazine on the grass in front of her.

Looking down, Jon caught a glimpse of her red lips stretched across the bulbous head of his cock and he shivered. She was taking her time, running her mouth up and down the shaft, sucking and licking at him as she would a giant lollipop.

Before he had met Melissa, he had always assumed that any relationship which used bondage, crops and canes to heighten the sexual pleasure was, by definition, a less than loving union. Melissa had shown him that quite the opposite was true. Though he loved to punish her upturned buttocks, to give her orders and see her cater to his every sexual whim, he also enjoyed taking care of her, cherishing her in a way that he had never felt able to cherish Ariane. Bathing her, washing her hair, massaging oils and creams into her skin – all these things were so intimate, they went beyond mere sex.

He liked it, too, when Melissa lavished her attention on him, as she was now, with no expectation of an immediate payback. He had never considered asking Ariane to serve him in that way, and yet there was so much pleasure to be had in massage and touch. Why had he never discovered that before?

He moaned softly as Melissa sucked rhythmically on his cock, drawing on the fount of sperm gathering at the base. He was going to come, any second now, and she would swallow it back without question, with enjoyment. She knew this triggered his release and he closed his eyes as he came, feeling totally and utterly at peace with himself.

It seemed to Ariane that she had been alone in the bedroom for hours, though common sense told her it could not be more than thirty minutes. Lying, spread-eagled on the navy blue satin bedspread, tied at her wrists and ankles by silk scarves, she felt exposed, totally at Conrad's mercy. Being deprived of her sight made her feel isolated and, if she was honest, not a little afraid.

And yet these feelings excited her. Probably as Conrad had intended, the ritual had served to heighten her anticipation for whatever was coming next. For the first few minutes she had lain, almost rigid with tension, the arousal churning through her, making her juices seep into the slippery satin of the duvet.

Now her arms and legs were beginning to cramp, her feminine secretions were drying on the surface of her skin where the warm air touched the open folds of her sex and she was beginning to think that Conrad wasn't coming back at all. She wouldn't put it past him to punish her by leaving her, bound and wanting, unfulfilled. Surely not – she couldn't bear it!

Lifting her head up as far as she could from the pillows, Ariane listened. As she had expected, there was no sound, nothing to penetrate the thick, velvety darkness surrounding her. She trembled. How much longer?

She jumped as the door to the hotel suite opened and closed. Every nerve in her body stretched taut as she strained to hear the sound of Conrad's footsteps crossing to the bedroom. There was nothing, only the unmistakable sense that she was no longer alone in the suite. Soon, it would begin.

It was then that she heard it – the unmistakable sound of another woman's laughter. Ariane stiffened, every muscle, every sinew held taut, listening. Though she couldn't make out what he was saying, she heard the low rumble of Conrad's voice, his tone teasing and seductive, and the woman laughed again, a low, rich sound that was more eloquent than any words.

What the hell was Conrad playing at? It sounded as though he had brought another woman back to the hotel and was about to seduce her in the living room while she was trussed to his bed in the room next door.

Pulling at the scarves that bound her, Ariane was frustrated to find that she couldn't get out of them. Furious and embarrassed, she opened her mouth and yelled.

'Conrad!'

For a moment there was no response, then she heard the door open and close softly. She gasped in surprise as she felt the palm of his hand stroke across her belly.

'What is it, Angel?'

'You . . . who is that with you in there?' she blurted, making no attempt to hide her indignation.

Conrad chuckled softly.

'Her name is Charlotte,' he told her.

The bed dipped under his weight as he sat down beside her. Tracing the contours of her face with one gentle finger, he continued, 'You'll like her. She's very pretty. Mid-twenties, long, soft blonde hair, not unlike yours, Angel,' he said, running his fingers through her hair and splaying it across the pillows.

'I don't want to see her!' Ariane said, horrified at the thought. 'You're not going to bring her in here, are you?'

Conrad caressed the soft, sensitive flesh of her lower lip, making her tremble with renewed desire. Then he ran his hand, palm down, along the length of her body, skimming over the leather straps that formed a pattern across it, from her throat, down between her breasts, over the soft flesh of her stomach until he reached her shaven mound. The purse of her sex, held open by the spread of her legs, was pushed out by the pressure of the straps running either side. Ariane held her breath as he touched the moist, open petals of flesh, so gently, making her clitoris quiver with anticipation.

'You have to learn self-control, my Angel. We don't have as much time as I thought, so I'm going to have to teach you the hard way.'

'What do you mean?' she whispered apprehensively.

'First, I'm going to take off the blindfold.'

Thank God for that, Ariane thought as he reached around her head and unfastened it. She blinked as the snug mask was peeled away, her eyes taking a few moments to adjust and focus.

Looking down, she saw how her breasts were moulded by the black leather harness, her nipples pressing lewdly through the gold rings constricting them. The thin straps around her upper thighs looked very black against her white skin, the inverted 'vee' which began below her navel framing the vulnerable paleness of her vulva as if it was a precious work of art.

Conrad tipped up her chin and kissed her on the forehead, on the cheeks and eyelids and, finally, at the very corner of her mouth.

'Are you uncomfortable?' he asked, trailing his fingers carelessly across her breasts.

'A little,' she admitted, not sure whether the admission would encourage him to relieve her discomfort, or increase it. To her relief, he chose the former.

'A change of position, I think.'

Ariane flexed her arms and legs as they were released, wincing as the blood began to flow more freely through her limbs. Conrad rubbed her wrists and ankles, his fingers gentle, soothing her.

'Sit up here,' he said, rearranging the pillows at the head of the bed so that she would be comfortable.

Ariane complied, curling her legs under her as he used one of the scarves to tie her hands loosely at the wrists behind her, leaving a sufficient length of scarf for him to loop around the bedpost. Ariane was tethered, though so loosely that it amounted to no more than a token bondage. Her entire body quivered with tension as she wondered what he would do next.

He smiled at her, and she saw in his eyes that he was aware of her apprehensive excitement, and approved of it. He seemed to be about to say something, but the door opened suddenly to reveal a model-perfect, pouting blonde vision of loveliness.

'You said you wouldn't be long, darling – oh!'

Catching sight of Ariane, the girl paused, running her eyes over her assessingly. It was clear that she wasn't surprised to find a semi-naked woman tied to the bedhead in Conrad's hotel bedroom, but she didn't seem particularly pleased, either. Ariane, for her part, was mortified, though she held the other woman's cool blue gaze proudly. She was damned if she was going to give her the satisfaction of knowing what a novice she was at these games!

Conrad caught her eye and, although he did not go so far as to smile at her, the expression in his eyes warmed and supported her. *You are the most important person in this room*, his eyes seemed to say to her. Turning to the other woman, still standing in the doorway, he introduced them.

'Angel, this is Charlotte. Charlotte – Angel.'

The vision of loveliness that was Charlotte seemed to make up her mind about something and she smiled. The smile transformed her face, lighting up her eyes and softening her features.

'I'm ver-ry pleased to meet you, Angel – Conrad has told me so much about you.'

*When*? Ariane wanted to ask, but she didn't get a chance. Charlotte covered the short distance between the doorway and the bed and leaned over to kiss Ariane firmly on the lips.

Ariane was so surprised that she didn't react at all. She stared straight ahead, her lips closed, her body rigid and unresponsive. Charlotte pulled back, a look of surprise on her lovely face.

'You didn't tell me she would be so . . . *undemonstrative*, darling,' she said, reaching out to caress Conrad's face.

Conrad shot an amused glance at Ariane.

'Don't worry about Angel, Charlotte – she responds when appropriate.'

Charlotte smiled back at him and a look passed between them that made Ariane feel totally and utterly excluded. It was not a pleasant feeling and she fidgeted awkwardly, pulling at her bonds. To her surprise, the silk scarf tightened around her wrists, holding her fast.

She watched helplessly as Conrad leaned across her to kiss Charlotte lingeringly on the lips, ignoring Ariane completely. What the hell did he think he was doing? Ariane could see his lips moving over the other woman's, was close enough to watch her part her lips and for his tongue to slip between them. They gave every appearance of being totally oblivious to Ariane: their eyes were closed, their bodies pressed as closely together as the space would allow.

As Ariane watched, horrified, Conrad reached across and began to fondle the other woman's breast beneath the soft, silk-satin vest she was wearing. At once she knew she could not bear to watch any more.

'Stop it!' she cried, so suddenly that they broke apart abruptly and turned to look at her.

Charlotte's pale blue eyes held a mild, condescending amusement that infuriated Ariane. Nevertheless, as she turned her attention to Conrad, she found herself wishing that amusement was what she could read in *his* eyes. He was angry with her, angry in that cold, cruel way that she dreaded. She could feel herself shrinking within herself as he addressed her.

'What did you say?'

Ariane found herself trying to reason with him, even while she knew she was wasting her time.

'I . . . I don't want to watch you make love to someone else. Please don't make me,' she begged.

Horribly conscious of Charlotte's mocking glance at her, Ariane focused all her attention on Conrad, pleading with him with her eyes not to humiliate her in this way. It was useless.

'Would you excuse us for a moment, Charlotte,' he said with a courteous smile in the other woman's direction.

Charlotte glanced from Conrad to Ariane and back again, assessing the situation.

'Of course,' she said. 'I'll go and open the champagne, shall I?'

'Yes – bring it in.'

He waited until Charlotte had walked through the door. It was only a matter of seconds, but to Ariane, whose heart was fluttering like the wings of a butterfly trapped in a net, it seemed to go on forever. She held her breath as Conrad slowly turned his head to look at her. He didn't say anything, merely looked at her with such coldness that he panicked her into ill-considered speech.

'I'm sorry, Conrad,' she blurted, 'but you know I want you to love me – *me*! How can I watch while you make love to a complete stranger?'

'You can because I wish it,' he said, his voice so cold and implacable that it made Ariane's blood freeze in her veins. Then he smiled and, somehow, that was much, much worse. 'Of course,' he said, *so* reasonably, 'I could untie you and call a cab. Is that what you prefer?'

The question hung in the air between them like a foul-smelling miasma. Ariane stared at Conrad, hating him for forcing her to make such a decision. Part of her wanted to spit in his face and tell him to hang his games on a rusty nail.

The other, far greater part, knew that she was curious, that she was not completely adverse to watching another couple make love in the same room. Somehow he knew of the voyeuristic side of her that she kept buried so deeply that she herself was only partially aware of its existence. Somehow, he knew how to divine her deepest, darkest fantasies, even the most shameful. *Especially* the most shameful.

Ariane shivered involuntarily as she realised, at last, the extent of the hold he had over her. Besides, despite that instant of hate, she trusted him to ultimately reward her.

'No,' she whispered, shaking her head so that her hair brushed softly against her cheeks. 'I want to stay. I'm sorry.'

Conrad stared back at her, his expression implacable. Ariane felt panic surge through her as she faced the possibility that he might make her go, anyway.

'Conrad?' she whispered.

He frowned, his eyes darkening as he stared at her.

'Do we always have to go through this charade? Every time I introduce you to something new, every little thing I ask you to do for me, we have to go through this pantomime of reluctance. We both know you will consent in the end, so why not cut the crap, just for once? Do you have any idea how much it bores me?'

Ariane stared at him, wide-eyed, cold fingers of dread playing up and down her spine. She couldn't bear it if he sent her away now. Faced with the possibility that he would, all her previous doubts and inhibitions seemed insignificant.

Impulsively, she leaned forward and pressed her cheek against the hand that lay in his lap.

'I'm sorry,' she whispered, shamefully aware that she was teetering on the brink of tears. 'I'll do what you say. I will, I promise. Only please don't send me away!'

He held her eye for a long, tension-filled moment.

'Do you mean that, Angel?' he asked softly.

'Oh yes,' she gushed with relief. 'I'll do anything, Conrad – anything you say!'

A part of her mind, the part that was still rational in spite of everything that had happened to her in the past few weeks, rang warning bells in her brain. Ariane chose, quite deliberately, to ignore them. Turning her face into Conrad's palm, she pressed her lips against the centre in a gesture of ardent submission, squeezing her eyes shut against the tears that were threatening to overflow.

# Ten

The tension in the room lengthened and thickened. Ariane wasn't sure exactly at what point it began to change, she was only glad that it did. Whereas before Conrad's anger and disappointment had lain heavy in the atmosphere, gradually it was replaced by a tension that was more sexual than angry.

Catching her chin between his thumb and forefinger, Conrad raised her face and kissed her gently on the lips.

'That's my Angel,' he murmured.

He touched her softly at the place where her labia met and Ariane felt her clitoris pulse immediately into life. Conrad smiled into her eyes, delighted now with her responsiveness.

'Be brave, Angel. I don't want you to come, do you understand?'

Ariane nodded mutely, wondering how he expected her to reach orgasm when her arms were tied behind her, her hands out of reach. He smiled approvingly at her.

'Good girl. Later, you will be allowed to come, and I promise you it will be one of the best orgasms you have ever had.'

'I've brought two glasses – Angel can share with us.'

The rare, tender moment which had stretched between them was shattered by the arrival of Charlotte bearing icy champagne. There was a subdued pop as she opened it and filled two long-stemmed flutes.

Ariane watched her, admiring her long, elegant fingers with their neatly manicured nails. She didn't like the way she had casually assumed that she too could call her 'Angel' – that was Conrad's name for her. Dutifully, she sipped from the glass that Conrad held to her lips, feeling the champagne bubbles fizz on her tongue.

Conrad and Charlotte drank deeply, flirting with their eyes over the rim of the flutes. This time, however, Ariane did not experience that dreadful sense of exclusion she had felt before, and she relaxed a little. She was aware of a change in the atmosphere in the room, a thickening of the air as Conrad and Charlotte moved further onto the bed. As if choreographed, they both set aside their glasses before moving into each other's arms.

They kissed again, more hungrily this time, kneeling up on the bed in front of Ariane so that their upper bodies were melded into one, inches away from her. Yet, as they caught fire it seemed as though Ariane was forgotten.

Strangely, this time she welcomed the cloak of anonymity which appeared to have descended around her. In its illusory embrace she was free to watch without being watched in her turn. She had never had occasion to see others making love, and her curiosity drove away any lingering feelings of doubt or shame.

Conrad's hands were roaming Charlotte's back, the fingers splaying against her shoulderblades as he pressed her closer. Ariane knew the feel of those hands, could empathise with the woman who was now moaning softly. As the kiss ended, Charlotte allowed her head to fall back so that her hair rippled like a golden waterfall down her narrow back and the tender white arc of her neck was exposed. Ariane felt a leap of desire as she watched Conrad press his lips against her throat.

Pushing Charlotte's top off her shoulders, he kissed the

exposed flesh, easing the strap of her bra down her upper arms so that the expanse of naked flesh was made wider. Ariane could see Charlotte's nipples pressing against the fabric of her bra and top, the shape delineated quite clearly.

As she watched, Conrad began to knead and caress her breasts, dipping his head to draw one tumescent nipple into his mouth, sucking on it through the material of her clothing. The silk satin darkened, the stain spreading outward from the centre of her breast.

Ariane felt her own nipples harden in response to the visual stimulus, swelling so that they pressed quite painfully against the unyielding metal of the gold rings surrounding them. She could almost imagine that it was *her* breast that he was kneading so tenderly, *her* nipple which he worried gently between his teeth, so closely did her own physical responses mirror those of Charlotte.

To her surprise, she found herself holding her breath as Conrad pulled the top up over Charlotte's head, wasting no time in removing her bra. The other woman's breasts, though not overly large, were firm and nicely shaped, the nipples and areolae a delicate shade of rose, rather small. She had a narrow ribcage, so that her breasts looked too heavy for her frame, and the kind of washboard stomach that can only be achieved by either voluntary starvation, or heredity.

She stood up on the bed so that Conrad could peel her minuscule skirt down her long, smooth legs. Once she had kicked off her shoes, she was left wearing nothing but a pair of wispy, white lace, high-leg panties which concealed very little. Ariane could see blonde wisps of hair curling around the edges and the pale pink flesh of her vulva was visible through the fabric, made diaphanous by the dampness where it had nestled into the folds of her sex

As Charlotte sank back down on the bed, Ariane caught a whiff of her perfume which, though very heavy and musky, could not conceal the richer, earthier scent of her arousal. To her shame, Ariane realised that she in her turn was aroused by this stimulus and, for the first time, she realised that it wasn't simply a matter of looking forward to seeing Conrad's naked body that had made her so willing to consent to this, his latest game.

Admitting to herself that she found Charlotte attractive was no mean achievement. She had never considered that she might be aroused by the sight of another woman's nakedness before and the revelation took some getting used to.

Running her eyes along the length of Charlotte's body, she found herself wondering what her skin would feel like under her fingertips. At close quarters it looked firm and springy, the golden surface smooth and soft.

As Ariane watched, Conrad stroked a path from her waist across her hip and down the slender length of her thigh, Charlotte sighed happily and wrapped her arms around his neck, pressing her upper body close to his. They were so close that Ariane could see the fine pores on the surface of the other woman's skin, could see the faint, betraying tremor of Conrad's hands as he cupped her breasts and, lifting them together, buried his face in the channel formed between them.

Charlotte meshed her fingers in his hair, moulding the shape of his skull and pressing him hard against her.

'Oh, Conrad – give it to me, darling! I want you inside me so badly!'

Glancing across at her over Charlotte's shoulder, Conrad caught Ariane's eye. She smiled faintly, relishing the brief moment of accord when he had signalled his distaste at Charlotte's rush. Ariane felt proud of her own, greater self control, prouder still of

Conrad's acknowledgement of it. *She* wouldn't demand that he take her at once, *she* would relish every moment of foreplay, enjoy the drawing out of the tension, content to allow Conrad to set the pace.

Silently, he climbed off the bed and began to unbutton his shirt. Both women watched him, Charlotte with hungry, lascivious eyes, Ariane with a sense of something long awaited, a treat to which she had looked forward for weeks.

He had a broad, well-muscled chest, the skin bronzed, smooth and hairless. His nipples were small and brown, puckering neatly as they were kissed by the air. Ariane's eyes dipped to the hard, flat planes of his stomach, aware that she was virtually holding her breath as he began to unbutton his trousers.

He had employed such rigid self-control for so long, she half expected to find that he was deficient in some way, maybe overly small, or disappointingly slender. Her eyes widened as she saw that he was not wearing any underpants and that, rising up from a thick, dark nest of wiry pubic hair was a more than adequate eight inches of sturdy cock, erect and ready for action.

She felt as if her heart rate had slowed to the point where she was conscious of every beat, as if she could actually feel the ebb and flow of the blood pumping through her veins. She hadn't expected him to be quite so . . . *beautiful*. Charlotte, on the other hand, clearly had no use for such aesthetic appreciation. Impatient, she crawled across the bed and fell on him, burying her face in his groin and opening her wide, luscious lips across the shiny, exposed knob of his glans.

Ariane's eyes darted from the sight of Conrad's cock disappearing and reappearing from Charlotte's mouth as she fellated him enthusiastically, to Conrad's face, and back again. She felt hot, her skin prickled where the perspiration pushed through her pores, and the tender flesh between her legs swelled and moistened. Aware of the dryness of her mouth and lips, she attempted to moisten them with her tongue.

She stopped short as she realised that Conrad's attention was focused, not on the woman sucking his cock, but the small movement of Ariane's tongue tip as it ran over her lips. At once, her temperature rose again. Her breasts swelled, her nipples pressing, on the verge of pain, against the restriction of the gold rings he had placed around them.

Conrad's expression was inscrutable, but intent as he watched her face. After a moment, he tangled his fingers in Charlotte's hair and pulled her gently away from him. Coaxing her up, onto her knees, he kneaded and stroked her breasts before, holding Ariane's eye, he took one rose-tipped breast into his mouth.

Ariane's gaze was locked with his as he sucked on the tumescent mound of flesh. His eyes were hot, boring into hers, as if trying to read her mind. Ariane was sure that it would not be difficult, that her feelings were written quite plainly across her face.

Jealousy was the emotion uppermost at that moment, not just because she wanted to be the owner of the breast that Conrad was suckling, but because she wished that hers was the mouth enclosing it.

Once he had read the desire on her face, Conrad turned his full attention to Charlotte, shutting her out. Ariane watched, feeling bereft and aroused in equal measure as Conrad lay Charlotte on the bed, easing her onto her back so that she lay in front of Ariane. She had to endure the sight of his lips and hands pleasuring her, roaming the smooth planes of her upper body with obvious relish.

Ariane's clitoris pulsed with a life of its own and she knew that, contrary to what she had thought before, it would be easy to come without touching herself. The fact that Conrad had forbidden her to do so was uppermost in her mind and she did not care to question his edict. Nevertheless, it was difficult to keep herself from tipping over the edge. Breathing shallowly, in through the nose, out through the mouth, she struggled to bring her riotous reactions under control.

The smooth, bronzed sweep of Conrad's back was so close, it was an agony not to be able to reach out and touch, to smooth the silken skin across the rigid iron of muscle and sinew. She could smell the clean, male tang of his skin and longed to taste the warm salt of the perspiration gilding the surface.

Slowly, as she watched, Conrad bent Charlotte's legs at the knees and eased them apart. Ariane's eyes widened as the pink, shiny folds of her sex were revealed.

She had never seen another woman's sex before, let alone smelled the earthy, mineral musk of female arousal. She could feel her own sex pulse with life, her clitoris beating like a tiny heart at the apex of her labia as her eyes ran across the neat, intricate folds of flesh.

'Beautiful, isn't it?' Conrad said, making her jump.

Ariane felt warm colour creep into her face as she realised that he had been watching her face, reading her reaction to the sight of Charlotte, spread before her.

'Wouldn't you like to kiss her – just here?'

He touched his fingertip gently against the hood of her clitoris and it slipped back to reveal the hard, shiny bead, making Charlotte groan.

'Imagine it, Angel – sliding your tongue along here, up to that pretty little bud, then down again to plunge it inside her . . .'

'No . . . !' Ariane moaned as he slid his finger inside Charlotte's vagina, stretching her, making her juices flow faster, running across his hand.

*What was he trying to do to her?*

'Conrad . . . please!' she begged, aware that her body teetered on the brink of orgasm, eased there by his seductive, shameful words.

She swallowed convulsively as, so slowly as to give his actions an almost theatrical flourish, Conrad dipped his head so that his face was inches from Charlotte's open sex. Putting out his tongue, he ran it lightly along the slippery channels of flesh, just as he had described, finally pushing inside the dark entrance to her body.

Ariane began to shake as he withdrew and she saw the other woman's dew glistening on his lips. To her horror, he leaned forward as if to kiss her.

'No!' she moaned, turning her head away.

Conrad caught her hair at the back of her head and forced her to look at him. Then slowly, holding her eye, he closed in on her, forcing his warm tongue between her lips and into the soft, warm recesses of her mouth.

Ariane could taste Charlotte's secretions on his tongue. They were sweeter than she had expected, discernible from Conrad's saliva by the heavier, thicker texture. Something throbbed, deep in her womb as she imagined drinking from Charlotte's body, the source of the honeyed nectar. Shocked by her own reactions, she pulled away, staring at him with wild, panic-filled eyes.

'Don't do this to me!' she begged.

All her life she had assumed she was firmly, *safely* heterosexual. Her own choice of adjectives struck even her as being odd, yet she clung to them like a woman drowning. To discover homosexual tendencies now challenged her very view of herself, making her feel confused and frightened.

Conrad read the panic in her eyes and kissed her again.

'Trust me, Angel,' he murmured as he drew away from her. 'Have I ever been wrong about you before?'

Ariane shook her head mutely, knowing that he was right, he had always known what she wanted, often before she had realised it herself. He smiled faintly at her, then turned his attention back to Charlotte, who was wiggling her hips restlessly, wanting more.

'Patience, my love,' Conrad said calmly.

Both women watched as he reached for his trousers and brought a condom out of the pocket. Unwrapping it, he glanced at Ariane and smiled.

'Would you put this on for me?' he asked her.

Ariane knew that her eyes lit up at the suggestion, but she didn't care how transparent her feelings might be, so long as he allowed her to touch him at last. Even performing this small service for him was better than being forced to look but not touch.

'Oh, yes,' she breathed, making him smile.

She trembled as he reached around her and untied the scarf around her wrists. Bringing both hands round to the front of her, he lifted them. Turning them over so that they were palm upward, he bent his head to kiss the delicate tracery of veins which patterned her inner wrists.

Ariane leaned into him, desperate to feel the warmth of his bare skin against hers, but he moved deftly out of her way, leaving her wanting. Without a word, he handed the condom to her and sat back on the bed.

His cock was straight, the circumcised tip soft and bulbous, but he wasn't fully erect. Ariane felt her mouth run dry as she contemplated it, unsure, suddenly, quite how to approach the task.

She was aware of Conrad's gaze on her. He raised his eyebrows at her hesitation and she reached for him, enclosing the thick, soft-skinned shaft of his penis in one hand whilst, with the other, she positioned the condom over the glans. To her delight, his cock stiffened at her touch and she took the time to stroke it, enjoying the way it swelled against her palm.

'Enough,' he said softly, but there was an edge to his voice which betrayed his own excitement. Ariane felt a surge of triumph at this evidence of how she had affected him. The condom unrolled slowly along his shaft and she held onto him a second more than was necessary, earning herself a warning glance from Charlotte.

Ariane ignored her. She didn't care about Charlotte, as far as she was concerned the other woman was merely another means by which Conrad had chosen to torment her, on a par with a crop, or a strap, or any of the other instruments of sweet torment to which he had introduced her. She only desisted at Conrad's signal, and even then reluctantly.

Something cramped in her belly as she watched him position the head of his cock at the entrance to Charlotte's body. Charlotte gave Ariane a triumphant smile as he pushed his way inside her. Ariane ignored Charlotte, all her attention was taken up with watching Conrad's face as he thrust into Charlotte's hungry body.

His expression was curiously intent, yet Ariane gained the distinct impression that his mind wasn't fully on what he was doing. Her suspicions were confirmed when he abruptly pulled out of the girl beneath him and turned to look at Ariane.

'Are you hot, Angel?' he asked, his voice low and resonant.

'Conrad—'

'Turn around, Charlotte,' he said, interrupting the other girl as she spoke.

'Yes, I'm hot,' Ariane admitted, hoping against hope that now he would turn to her; that, at last, she was to receive that which she had desired for so long.

'Are you wet?'

Though she didn't need to touch herself to reply in the affirmative, Ariane reached between her legs and, holding Conrad's eye, entered her body with two fingers. She watched his eyes darken, drawn irresistibly to the centre of her femininity and she felt a rush of power. Slowly, she withdrew her fingers and held them up for his inspection.

'Oh, yes,' she murmured throatily, 'I'm very wet.'

She saw a new expression in Conrad's eyes, a dawning respect that made her feel exultant. *He is as much in thrall to me as I am to him*, she thought, holding his gaze. At last, she understood. *Which of us is it that has the power – which is the dominant and which the submissive?*

'Good,' he said at last, his voice low and silky. 'Sit at the top of the bed,' he instructed her, 'and spread your legs wide.'

Ariane did so willingly, pressing her back against the headboard and allowing her heels to slip on the cool satin of the bedspread, opening herself to him. It was some minutes before she realised his intention.

He had climbed off the bed and walked round to the end of it, his cock jutting in front of him, the condom shiny with Charlotte's juices. Charlotte had turned to face Ariane, a cat-like smile on her lovely face that Ariane did not trust. She was kneeling up on the bed so, for the moment, Ariane could not see Conrad's face.

'Make her come, Charlotte,' he said quietly.

Ariane's eyes widened in horror as she realised what was about to happen. Before she could move to close her legs, Charlotte buried her head into her crotch and began lapping at the moist, distended folds of flesh around her open sex.

'No! Oh, no, I—'

'Let it come, Angel,' Conrad said, his voice slipping like silk across her heated senses.

'But I *can't*!' she cried desperately, her mind rebelling against the unmistakable building of sensation in the depths of her womb. 'Please, Conrad – don't make me! Not this . . . I can't, I *can't*!'

'Do it for me, Angel,' he said.

As he spoke, he lifted Charlotte by the hips so that her firm, rounded bottom was presented to him. As Ariane watched, he eased her knees apart. Then, his eyes boring into Ariane's, he entered Charlotte from behind.

The other woman murmured appreciatively, the sound muffled by Ariane's body. She licked with renewed enthusiasm at Ariane's soaking sex flesh, causing her clitoris to swell and harden to the point of discomfort.

As Conrad thrust in and out of her, he held Ariane's eye and she realised that he was using Charlotte as a channel by which he could make love to her. The orgasm which, she could see from the tension in his face, was building up within him was for her, just as her climax when it came would be for him.

*Do it for me.* Ariane wasn't sure whether he had said the words aloud again or if she was just remembering, and she didn't care. All she *did* know was that Charlotte's relentless tongue was forcing her closer and closer to the edge, lashing her clitoris with increasing ferocity until she thought she would faint with the sheer pleasure of it.

'Yes!' Conrad hissed.

His eyes had grown opaque and Ariane realised that, though he was still staring straight at her, he no longer saw her at all. He was close to coming and his imminent climax gave Ariane's inexorable race to fulfilment a spur. She could feel a hot flush creeping up from her waist, travelling across her breasts and suffusing her neck and face with warm colour. Even her toes tingled as the first waves of pleasure broke over her.

The veins were showing at Conrad's temples. As Ariane watched, a bead of sweat ran slowly down the side of his face. Reaching his climax, he held Charlotte's hips firmly and thrust into her more deeply, making her squeal against the convulsing flesh of Ariane's vulva.

Conrad opened his eyes wide and stared at Ariane, so that it seemed to her that they reached the peak together.

After a few minutes, he withdrew from Charlotte, helping her to sit up and pulling her against him so that he was supporting her.

'Poor Charlotte!' he crooned, reaching down to touch her neglected sex.

Still breathing heavily, Ariane watched as he opened it like a flower, revealing the tender, darker pink membranes inside. They were slick with her juices and she moaned as Conrad moved his fingers across the stretched flesh, circling her clitoris with his fingerpad.

Charlotte's labia pouted like a small mouth, her clitoris pulsing gently beneath Conrad's fingers. Her vagina was spread apart and, overcome by an urge she did not take the time to analyse, Ariane reached out and slipped her fingers inside the moist, shadowed cleft.

At once, Charlotte's muscles spasmed, clutching at Ariane's fingers as she moved them in and out of her.

'Yes, oh yes – harder!' she moaned, trapping Ariane's hand between her strong thighs.

The convulsing flesh of Charlotte's vagina drew Ariane's fingers in deeper, encouraging her to explore the hot, silken passage. Conrad leaned forward and kissed Ariane hard, on the mouth. The kiss went on and on, until Charlotte lay panting against Conrad's chest, crushed between them.

Ariane opened her eyes and found herself staring straight into Conrad's. Her breath caught in her chest as she saw the expression in his eyes. The woman crushed between them was forgotten as Ariane basked in the warmth of his approval, knowing that, had he asked her, at that moment she would have done anything for him.

'Well, guys, it's been a ball, but I have to go now.'

Wrenched rudely from their mutual absorption, both Conrad and Ariane greeted Charlotte's cheery announcement with confusion. Conrad was the first to recover.

'Do you want me to call you a cab?' he asked, watching as she dressed.

'I can see to it – you stay here. Good to meet you, Angel. 'Bye, darling – look me up sometime, okay?'

They waited until she had left them alone before turning towards each other again. Without a word, Conrad unstrapped the harness around Ariane's body before removing the gold rings around her nipples by sucking each one into his mouth. Ariane felt desire stir again in the pit of her belly, and she reached for him, eager to feel his penis swell once again in her hand. With a small, regretful smile, he stopped her.

'No, Angel. It's time for you to go.'

Ariane stared at him, hoping she had misunderstood.

'But *why*?' she pleaded when she saw he would not be swayed.

Conrad smoothed her hair back from her face in a gesture so tender it brought weak tears to her eyes.

'Haven't you worked it out yet?' he asked her softly.

'What? I don't understand!'

Conrad held her eye as he searched for the right words.

'I am not the other half to your other. Think of me as your tutor. Only Jon has the right to possess you totally.'

'Jon? But how can I continue to live with Jon after this? Are you saying I won't see you again?' She was appalled by how much the prospect hurt her.

'Probably not. Don't look so stricken, Angel. There's still tomorrow.'

'Tomorrow?' she whispered.

'Yes. Tomorrow you will have the chance to show how much you really love me.'

'And if I do – won't you make love to me, just once?'

A shutter seemed to come down over Conrad's eyes as she pleaded with him and Ariane felt the familiar, delicious thrill of danger dart through her.

'Perhaps,' he said tonelessly.

And that had to be enough.

# *Eleven*

'To conclude, ladies and gentlemen, I think you will now agree that to proceed with the plans for Jensen Electronics in their current form, simply isn't a viable option.'

Jon watched Melissa as she paused, giving the assembled executives a chance to absorb the thrust of her argument. It had been a convincing one, and Jon hoped she would be given the opportunity to outline the alternative strategy she had devised.

It would all depend on the reaction of the chairman, a redoubtable septuagenarian with iron-grey hair and an alarmingly wide-shouldered business suit. Her long, scarlet-painted fingernails tapped thoughtfully on the pad in front of her and, though no-one was looking directly at her, Jon was aware that all were waiting for her to speak.

'That was very convincingly argued, Miss Taylor,' she said at last in a voice honed over many years on Marlboros and bourbon. 'I take it that you do have an alternative suggestion to put to us?'

Melissa smiled, her dark eyes flickering briefly towards Jon, sharing her triumph with him.

'Yes, Mrs Devlin, if I may . . . ?'

The chairman nodded as Melissa indicated that she wished to use the flip pad set up in the corner of the board room. Once given the go-ahead, she walked confidently over to it and, uncapping a marker pen, began to outline her proposal.

Jon allowed the sound of her voice to wash over him without trying to listen to her words. He knew what she was going to say, anyway – the night before they had rehearsed her spiel until she was word perfect, every pause, every nuance carefully planned for maximum effect. Melissa would have her idea adopted, of that he had no doubt. It was too good to be overlooked.

He watched her as she spoke, her lovely face animated with enthusiasm. Glancing at the chairman, he saw that she, too, was impressed with Melissa's vivacity, though, unlike Jon, she was also listening carefully to what she had to say.

Jon was keener to look than listen. This morning, Melissa was wearing a sky-blue skirt suit with a crisp white blouse underneath. The blouse had a small, neat, pointed collar and fold-back cuffs that showed beneath the sleeves of the lightweight jacket. The skirt was narrow, but not too tight, the hemline ending just above her knees. Her long, slender legs were encased in silky, flesh-toned stockings, almost exactly the same colour as her high-heeled suede court shoes.

'Do I look all right?' she had asked him earlier as he lay in bed at her apartment and watched her dress.

'Gorgeous!' he had replied truthfully.

'Not too gorgeous – I want to be taken seriously.'

'Put your hair up, then,' he suggested, eyeing her flowing locks with pleasure.

Sitting in front of the mirror, Melissa arranged her hair so that it lay close against her head in a French plait. Fastening the end with a covered band, she gathered up the ends of the plait and hid them with a dark blue velvet pouch which caught the light when she moved.

Jon had watched her in the mirror as she applied her make-up.

As she traced the outline of her full lips with a lip pencil, then loaded a brush with lipstick, he felt his cock rise with remembered pleasure. She turned to him when she had finished and gave him a twirl.

'*Voilà*! I'm ready.'

'Not quite.'

Jon saw the surprise in her face as he sat up on the bed, and was glad he had managed to put it there.

'What do you mean?' Her voice held that heavy, husky quality it always held when she was aroused and he knew that he had perfected the art of catching her attention with his voice. He only had to speak to her in a certain tone, look at her in a certain way, and she was reduced to a quivering mass of desire.

'I have a present for you. I'd like you to wear it today, to bring you luck.'

Melissa's face lifted in a smile and she went over to sit down beside him on the bed. Jon guessed that she assumed he had bought her a brooch or a bracelet or some other conventional trinket and he smiled inwardly, anticipating her surprise. It felt good to be able to show her that he had learned so much from her in their time together that now he was quite capable of initiating a game on his own.

'What is it?'

Jon reached into the drawer beside the bed and pulled out the small gold-coloured bag. He had happened on a small shop above a bakery near the office the day before. While Melissa spent her lunch hour working on her presentation, Jon had gone out for a walk, conscious that this would be the last time in a while that he would be in New York. He had been delighted to happen upon the treasure trove of erotica above the bakery. So many jewels in such a mundane setting had added to the thrill.

179

'Stand up,' he said. 'Now – take off your panties.'

'Take off my . . . Jon, I can't go to work without panties on!'

'Of course you can.'

'But today of all days . . .' she trailed off and, holding Jon's eye, lifted her skirt to comply with his request.

Her eyes widened as he tipped the gold bag upside down so that two small silver balls, connected by a fine chain, dropped into his palm.

'Chinese love balls?'

He nodded.

'Exquisite, aren't they?' he said, holding them up so that they glinted in the early morning light. 'I had our initials engraved, one on each ball – see?' He showed her the 'J' and the 'M' marked in elaborate, curlicued script, one initial in the centre of each ball. 'I thought it would be something you could remember me by.'

Melissa seemed to be unable to tear her eyes away from them, but she shook her head.

'I don't think—'

'Come here.'

She obeyed him, standing acquiescent as he began to caress the soft strip of flesh between her stocking top and her sex. Slowly, watching her face, he edged towards the tender places concealed between her closed legs. He heard the tenor of her breathing change, become shallower and more rapid and he leaned forward so that he could place a kiss on her shaven mons.

The unmistakable, musky scent of her arousal told him that when he sank his fingers into the sensitive cleft, he would find her moist and swollen. He loved the way she became aroused so quickly. Mere minutes ago she had been talking about her presentation, thinking of the image she needed to project in the boardroom. Now, it seemed, all thought of work had fled from her mind as she waited for him to touch her.

Jon did not keep her waiting for long. Reaching for her, he parted the tender folds of flesh, just enough to give his tongue access to the sweetness within. She sighed as he ran the very tip of his tongue along her slit, wiggling it in deeper so that he could probe the dark entrance to her womb.

A small sigh of submission escaped through her lips and she shuffled her feet apart, widening the opening, luring his tongue in deeper.

Jon felt a deep sense of satisfaction as he tongued her. No matter what happened when he was back in London, this time he had spent with Melissa would live on in his memory as a golden interlude. He could feel her sex flesh quivering against his tongue and knew that it would soon begin to throb and pulse as her orgasm flowed through her. It took a good deal of self-control to make himself pull away just as she reached the brink.

'Oh, no!' she moaned.

The expression in her eyes told him that she knew exactly why he had pulled back and he smiled at her.

'Oh, yes,' he said, kissing her gently on the mouth.

Picking up the silver balls he rolled them in his palm. They made a small clinking sound as they collided and Melissa's eyes widened.

'People will be able to hear them,' she protested half-heartedly.

'If you wear those suede courts you laid out last night they'll assume any sound is the tap of your heels against the floor. Besides, the assistant assured me that they'll only roll together inside you if you set up a momentum. You'll have to be careful how you walk.'

Indicating that she should sit on the bed, Jon eased her thighs apart. For a moment he simply admired the contours of her sex, looking forward to seeing them again when they arrived home that evening.

'We have to leave soon,' she reminded him gently. 'I don't want to be late today.'

He smiled at her, toying with the idea of keeping her here until her lateness would be inevitable. Maybe he should send her to work with fresh stripes bisecting the delicious peach of her bottom . . . Deciding that such action would be too cruel, he pressed the silver balls against the lip of her vagina.

Melissa moaned as he eased the first ball inside her, pushing it gently up the elastic-walled channel until it met the resistance of her cervix. He gazed at her for a moment, enjoying the sight of the silver chain emerging from her vagina with the second ball attached. If he had had the time, he would have photographed her like that, for the sight was bizarrely beautiful, quite moving. It would certainly add to her portfolio.

Realising that time really was now running short, he introduced the second ball into her body, feeling it knock against the first, making her suck in her breath.

'All right?' he murmured against her hair.

Melissa nodded, so, making sure that a loop of silver chain still protruded from her body, Jon smoothed her skirt back over her hips and reluctantly turned his attention to getting himself ready for work.

Now he watched her as she sold her idea to the chairman and the other members of the board and he felt a surge of admiration for her. Though she must be supremely conscious of the silver balls rolling inside her, Melissa gave no sign of any discomfort, moving and speaking with self-assured confidence.

Jon glanced around at his colleagues. What did they see when they looked at Melissa? Trying to look at her objectively, he attempted to see her as they did. He saw a lovely, self-assured young woman whose intelligence outshone even her beauty. She was dressed attractively, but not overtly so, and her neatly plaited hair spoke of her desire to be taken seriously on a business level.

So much for how the others saw her. Had any of them noticed, he wondered, the slight colour in her cheeks that wasn't due to make-up, or the brightness of her eyes which could not be caused even by her unquestionable enthusiasm for her argument? Did they see the way she moved, so carefully so as not to roll her hips, the way in which she continually moistened her lips with a discreet tongue tip whenever she paused for breath.

Oh, no, Melissa, you're by no means unaffected by my gift, he told himself with satisfaction. Had she come yet? Or were the balls keeping her just on the brink, making the adrenalin pump continuously through her veins, probably indirectly affecting the performance she was giving so brilliantly.

Under the table, he pressed his hand against the painful constriction at his groin and undressed her with his eyes. Later, when they got back, he would make her bend over the dining table while he pushed his cock into the tight, hot tube of her anus. He would feel the Chinese love balls rock against each other, separated from his penis only by the thinnest of membranes.

The idea was making him feel hot all over. Maybe he wouldn't have to wait until they got home, maybe they could book into a cheap hotel during the lunch hour . . .

Startled out of his contemplation by the breaking out of applause, Jon joined in, realising from the universal smiles that Melissa's presentation had been a success. Joining the throng who moved to congratulate her once the chairman had retired,

Jon put his lips against her hair and whispered, 'Well done, sweetheart. Did my gift help?'

'Like a lucky charm,' she replied out of the corner of her mouth.

Her eyes were glazed with arousal and Jon was hard-pressed to conceal his erection from the others.

'Executive washroom, half an hour,' he told her.

She nodded and he slipped quietly away to fetch the items he would need.

Melissa's eyes were so bright when she arrived that, if he hadn't known better, Jon would have said she had a fever. Glancing around to check that no one had seen them, she virtually fell on Jon the moment the door was locked behind them.

'Into the stall,' he told her. 'Bend over the toilet bowl.'

He had no time for foreplay and it seemed that Melissa had no need of it. Pulling up her skirt, she exposed her rounded bottom to him and braced herself with her hands flat on the closed lid of the toilet.

'I didn't think I was going to be able to wait,' she gasped as he unzipped his trousers. 'I've been going crazy!'

'Me, too. Spread your legs wider.'

In his pocket he had a tube of lubricating cream and a condom. Melissa squealed as he pressed the nozzle of the tube into her bottom and squeezed out its contents.

'God, that's cold!'

'It'll soon warm up. Can you hold it?'

Realising it took some skill to hold the cream inside her, ready for him, he stroked the small of her back and the rounded globes of her buttocks, waiting for her consent.

'Yes,' she said through gritted teeth, 'but I don't know how much longer I can hold onto the balls.'

'Oh, but you must,' Jon said silkily, nudging the forbidden

orifice with the tip of his cock. 'I want to feel them . . . ahh! You're so tight . . . so hot!'

Melissa pushed her bottom back against him, easing his entry. For a moment he simply rested inside her, enjoying the sensation of filling her while the silver balls rolled against his cock through the walls of her vagina. It was like nothing he had ever felt before and he knew it wouldn't be long before he came.

'I can't hold back,' he warned her.

Reaching around her, he rubbed at the slippery bead of her clitoris. Melissa came at once, grinding her hips against his belly as her vaginal muscles contracted, setting the balls clicking wildly together. The combined stimulation tipped Jon over the edge and he came with a shout, the hot fluid pumping out of him in urgent, violent jags.

Then it was over. The balls slipped into Melissa's cupped hand as he pulled out of her. White cream oozed from her back passage and he cleaned her up, dropping the used tissue paper with the condom in the toilet bowl. They kissed, then parted, each going to their separate offices as if nothing had happened.

Later that day, Jon heard that Melissa's proposals had been accepted. He also received the tickets for their flight to London the following morning. One more night of celebration, then he was going to have to face real life, in the form of Ariane, back home.

Ariane woke the morning after the session with Conrad and Charlotte, alone in the bed she normally shared with Jon, and yawned. Stretching lazily, she considered rising. After a shower and something to eat, she might not feel quite so limp. Maybe she could even get on with some work.

Then again, she thought, burrowing deeper into the duvet,

she could just roll over and go back to sleep. The harmless indulgence was rudely interrupted by the buzzing of the doorbell. Once she had been forced to conclude that the visitor was not going to go away, she hauled herself reluctantly from the bed and went to answer the door.

It was Conrad.

'What on earth are you doing here?' she asked him, aware that she looked sleepy and dishevelled, her appearance far removed from the casual neatness of his.

'I thought we'd spend the rest of the day together,' he told her, making his way through to the living room.

Ariane followed him, admiring the shape of his buttocks beneath the heavy black denim of his jeans. He was wearing a black shirt, too, tucked in at the waist, and slim-toed black leather boots.

'Make yourself at home – I'll go and get some clothes on.'

'Some of these are very good.'

She hesitated as he picked up one of her sketches and examined it in the light of the window. It was a full frontal shot of herself, recognisable, she was sure, even though she had drawn her arm thrown across her face. She was naked and her nipples had been pierced by two gold rings. Lying on her back, she had a generous bunch of grapes balanced at the apex of her thighs, concealing the naked fruit of her sex.

'Thank you,' she said quietly, watching his face. As she watched him, he traced the outline of the nipple rings lightly with his fingertips. Ariane felt her own nipples harden in response.

He looked up suddenly and smiled at her.

'Jon flies in tomorrow – with Melissa.'

'Tomorrow?'

'Yes. I have to leave on Tuesday. It could be . . . interesting, don't you think, for the four of us to spend some time together?'

Ariane stared at him, her sleep-fuddled mind wrestling with the implications of what he had said.

'Jon didn't say he was coming back early,' she said.

'I don't think he knew until recently.'

'Is there something wrong?'

'On the contrary, I hear he's done such a damn good job that he's finished early. There's nothing to be gained by sticking out the full term simply for the sake of it.'

'Does he know . . . about you and I?'

Conrad crossed the short distance between them and took her in his arms. Kissing her gently on the lips, he avoided her question.

'It's inevitable that you'll notice changes in each other,' he said obliquely.

Ariane knew her whole attention should be focused on thinking about her fiancé's imminent return, but Conrad's nearness made it impossible for her to think about anything at all.

'Now,' he was saying as he turned her towards the bedroom, 'you said something about getting dressed? Let me run you a nice hot bath.'

Ariane allowed him to steer her into the bedroom. She watched him through the open doorway as he ran the bath, whistling Dixie softly through his teeth. He seemed to be in a happy mood, but then, of course, Melissa would be arriving with Jon in the morning. Had he missed her?

'It's ready,' he told her.

As if on automatic pilot, Ariane stepped out of her nightdress and walked, naked, into the bathroom. She had become used to him bathing her, attending to all her intimate needs and she lay back in the warm water with a sense that she had left all right to independent thought at the bathroom door. Rather than making her feel imprisoned, she found the concept a liberating one, and she prepared to empty her mind and relax.

It was curiously soothing to have someone else soap her, massaging her tenderly, polishing her skin with soap. Conrad lathered her hair with shampoo, piling it up high on her head before rinsing it with the showerhead. Meanwhile, he smeared a sweet-smelling face pack across her face, wiping it off tenderly with cotton wool after the prescribed time.

The moisturiser he massaged into her face smelled divine, as did the expensive potion he poured into the water from a small glass vial. Little globules of oil formed on the surface of the water and Ariane lay back and relaxed, imagining it coating her skin.

When the water began to cool, Conrad blotted her skin dry with thick, fluffy towels which he had warmed over the radiator. Dusting her from top to toe in talcum powder, he led her over to the bed, telling her to lie on her back on the dry towels he had lain across it.

Ariane forced herself to relax as he shaved and oiled her vulva, trying desperately hard to ignore the pulse that beat steadily in her sex as he lingered over the silky flesh of her inner lips. Conrad's eyes told her that he knew how much it cost her to hang on to her self-control, and she was proud of herself for achieving it.

'Roll over now,' he said softly when he had finished.

As she turned her head to one side and closed her eyes, Ariane reflected that there was rarely anything sexual about his touch when he bathed her, his whole concentration seemed to be focused on caring for her. Now he began to massage her shoulders and her back, sending little messages of bliss along her nerve endings.

'Mmm, that's lovely!' she murmured.

'Ssh! Just relax. Close your eyes and I'll tell you what we're going to do on our last night together.'

Deliberately ignoring his allusion to the fact that their relationship would soon be over – she would have time enough to think of that later – Ariane smiled, eager to hear what new games he had devised for her. She stiffened as he spoke.

'You've done *what*?' she whispered, horrified.

'I've arranged to loan you to two friends,' he repeated patiently. 'Don't be alarmed – I'll be in the room all the time.'

Was that supposed to reassure her?

'But I don't want to do it, Conrad! I'll feel like a prostitute!'

'You needn't, since there won't be any money changing hands. Don't let's go through this whole charade of reluctance again. You know how wearisome I find it.'

Ariane realised he meant what he said, but she couldn't believe he would ask her to do something that was so alien to her moral integrity.

'Conrad . . . you have to understand, before I met you I was faithful to Jon. I've never done anything like this before . . .'

She sighed as he began to stroke his oiled fingers along the sensitive crease of her bottom. Gradually, he caressed her more deeply, his fingertips edging towards the moist purse of her sex.

'I know you haven't, Angel – that's what makes it all so exciting! Don't you enjoy seeing how far your inhibitions can break down?'

'Yes,' she admitted reluctantly, opening her legs to allow him easier access to the heated folds of flesh. 'But to do it with a stranger, never mind two—'

'Would be an unforgettable experience. You'll love it, Angel, I promise you. Trust me.'

His fingers thrummed against the small promontory of her

189

clitoris and Ariane sighed as a gentle orgasm flowed over her. She was never able to deny him anything when he treated her like this, and he knew it. His low, persuasive words were more potent than any spanking, or darker coercion might have been.

'All right,' she sighed, closing her legs around his hand. 'But promise you'll stay with me.'

'I promise, sweet Angel,' he murmured.

She felt his lips press against her bare shoulder and she turned her face to look at him. He smiled at her.

'Remember – you're only acting a part,' he said.

Ariane raised her eyebrows. She supposed he was right, really. In all their games she allowed herself to assume a rôle, a means to an end.

'I've brought the clothes I want you to wear. First, though, I wonder if you'd do a favour for me?'

Ariane sat up, intrigued.

'Anything.'

'You have a great deal of talent as an artist. Do you think you could produce a drawing of me like those in your living room for Melissa?'

Ariane smiled, surprised at the request.

'I'd be glad to – but only if you'll consent to my keeping the sketches for myself.'

Conrad kissed her on the lips.

'Of course. Would you like to set things up while I make us some brunch?'

He cooked them eggs and bacon, sausage and tomato. Ariane hadn't realised how hungry she was until she finished mopping her plate with a slice of bread, earning herself an amused glance from Conrad. Afterwards he took off his clothes and allowed Ariane to pose him against the pillows on her bed.

She made several sketches of him from different angles. Having him lie on his stomach with his head turned away from her, she described the long, lean length of his back and the firm muscles in his buttocks. On his side, she captured his full frontal beauty, then she made various lightning sketches of him on his back, his long hair flowing over his face.

All these line drawings she would keep for herself. For Melissa, she chose to sketch him staring straight at the observer, so that his dark eyes would seem to follow them from whatever vantage point his portrait would be hung. Concentrating on perspective, she had him lean on his elbows, delineating every line and crease of his stomach lovingly as he half-sat, half-lay on the bed.

After his eyes, which established the dominance that was so much a part of his character, she decided that the gaze should be drawn to his cock, now sleeping at his groin. After asking Conrad to pose for half an hour while she made the original sketch, she took her time to complete the drawing.

Once she had detailed every hair, every shadow to her satisfaction, she showed the drawing to Conrad. He took it from her and was silent as he surveyed it.

'Angel, you have real talent,' he said, a respect colouring his tone that made her feel warm inside.

'Will Melissa like it, do you think?'

'I'm sure she will. You ought to do more of this sort of thing, Angel – with your eye for detail you could become very successful as an erotic artist.'

Ariane flushed with pleasure at his praise.

'Thank you,' she said. 'I'll certainly think about it. Is it time to get ready to go out yet?'

Glancing at the clock she saw that it was five o'clock already. Time had flown past, so absorbed had she been in her drawing, and she was looking forward to dinner.

Conrad, too, seemed surprised to see the time. After helping Ariane to clear away her equipment, he went down to fetch the clothes he had brought her from the car.

'Oh, Lord!' Ariane exclaimed as he opened the box and took out the dress he expected her to wear.

Conrad smiled.

'Lovely, isn't it? Take off your clothes.'

Ariane complied, standing obediently in front of him as he eased the dress over her head and smoothed it down her body. She could see herself in the mirrored door of the wardrobe, hardly recognisable as herself.

The dress was bright red, made from an apparently seamless tube of cotton and lycra. It had a deeply scooped neck and wide straps which could be worn on or off the shoulder. Running her eyes downward, she saw that it clung like a second skin to every detail of her naked body, and ended a mere inch below the exposed flesh of her mons.

Conrad knelt at her feet and, lifting each one, rolled sheer, flesh-toned stockings up her legs. Using old-fashioned elastic garters to hold them up, he then lifted her feet again and fitted them into ludicrously high-heeled sandals, the same pillarbox red as the dress.

Ariane stared at her reflection, barely recognising the image gazing back at her.

'Fairly heavy make-up, I think. And we'll curl your hair.'

Coming up behind her, he folded his arms around her, holding her eye in the mirror as he bent his head to kiss the dip of her collarbone.

'You look like a high-class hooker,' he told her. 'Rupert and Andrew won't be able to believe their luck!'

Ariane felt the apprehension shiver along her spine, though this time she welcomed it, knew that the sinking feeling she was experiencing now was usually a prelude to untold pleasure. Remembering his half-formed promise of the night before, she pressed her lips against his forearm.

'Will you . . . love me yourself if I do what you want me to do with Rupert and Andrew?' she could not help herself asking.

In the mirror, she saw Conrad's expression change. He looked almost frighteningly remote, his eyes unreadable as he looked at her.

'No bargaining, Angel. It's time to leave.'

She wanted to press him, but one look at his face told her that he would not be pressed. Using her nervousness to propel her forward, she followed him out of the flat.

Rupert and Andrew were waiting for them at a smart restaurant on the south bank of the river. Rupert was tall, over six feet, with floppy blond hair and a slightly vacant expression which, Ariane soon concluded, was an affectation rather than the physical manifestation of a personality trait.

Andrew was older, possibly in his mid-forties, of a similar height and build to Conrad. His thick, dark hair was greying attractively at the temples, cut close to his scalp at the sides, but longer on the top. Both men were formally dressed and greeted her with impeccable manners.

'Good to meet you, Angel,' Andrew said once he had been introduced.

Ariane smiled and shook the hand he held out to her, finding his grip warm and firm. His eyes assessed her, but not in a cold way, and she felt her skin prickle under his scrutiny.

Rupert's regard, on the other hand, was hot and uncomfortable, his eyes never leaving her bust as she was introduced to him.

Disconcerted, Ariane pressed closer to Conrad. Splaying his fingers against the small of her back, he indicated that she should take the seat Andrew had pulled out for her.

Though they did not deliberately exclude her, Ariane did not contribute much to the conversation as they ate dinner. Finding that her appetite had deserted her, she toyed with her food, trying to ignore Rupert's persistent leering.

Under the table, Conrad caressed her stockinged thighs, his fingers straying frequently to the exposed, newly depilated skin of her mons and vulva. In this way, he kept her constantly on the brink of orgasm, so that she was supremely conscious of her body, and of the effect that it was having on the three men with her.

Impulsively, she placed her hand on Conrad's cock, satisfying herself that he was as aroused as she was. He removed her hand at once. Leaning forward, he whispered in her ear, 'You'll pay for that.'

His words thrilled her, set up that deep, dark trembling that always preceded the best of their games. Feeling Andrew's eyes on her, she looked up and was caught in the intensity of his gaze. His eyes were iron-grey, curiously opaque as he looked at her. Ariane felt something trip in her chest and knew at once that here was a man to be reckoned with.

Glancing uncertainly at Conrad, she saw that he was watching Andrew carefully. From his expression, she realised that he was pleased with what he saw in the older man's face.

'I must congratulate you, Conrad, on your taste,' Andrew said after a few moments. He raised his glass in a silent toast to Ariane as he talked to Conrad about her. 'Is she trained?'

'Yes, although, naturally, I don't expect you to take my word for it,' Conrad answered, signalling for more wine.

Andrew moistened his lips with the tip of his tongue. He was looking at Ariane, but, whereas before he had been charming, now she had the strangest feeling that he wasn't seeing her at all. She didn't like the way they were discussing her, as if she couldn't hear them. Glancing towards the silent Rupert, she saw that he was finding it hard to conceal his arousal. His pale complexion had turned pink and perspiration had broken out across his forehead.

They all had more wine, then Andrew seemed to make his mind up about something.

'We'll travel by cab to my apartment,' he announced. Then, for the first time since they had arrived, he addressed Ariane directly.

'Come, my dear,' he said, rising and holding out a hand to her. 'Let us put you through your paces.'

His odd choice of words made her shiver. She had to swallow at the lump that had suddenly formed in her throat before she put out her hand. As Andrew's warm fingers enclosed hers, she rose.

Glancing uncertainly at Conrad, he nodded almost imperceptibly at her. Taking a deep breath, Ariane walked with Andrew out of the restaurant, leaving Conrad to follow with Rupert.

# Twelve

Jon and Melissa arrived at the airport feeling decidedly jaded.

'I'll go straight to the hotel while you go home, Jon,' she suggested as they waited to collect their baggage. 'We both need to rest.'

'Okay. I'll find a cab and drop you at your hotel first – it's not far out of my way.'

Melissa smiled at him wickedly, and at once he forgot his weariness.

'Great – I know a wonderful way of taking your mind off the jet-lag!'

Finding a cab, Jon gave the driver his instructions and sat back in his seat. As soon as the car drew away from the curb, Melissa began to caress his thigh through the thin fabric of his chinos.

'What are you doing?' he said softly, so that the driver wouldn't hear.

'One last blow-job?' she suggested, laughing lightly as she saw the effect her unexpectedly direct proposition had on the bulge in his trousers.

'For Christ's sake, Melissa!' Jon protested half-heartedly, conscious of the taxi driver watching them in his rear-view mirror.

Melissa ignored him, deftly unbuttoning his fly and scooping his rising cock out of his underpants. Even if he had felt inclined to continue to protest, he wouldn't have had the time, for Melissa was already drawing him into the heated interior of her mouth, swirling her tongue around the rim of his glans as if tasting the most exquisite delicacy.

Leaning back in his seat, Jon closed his eyes and resigned himself to bliss. God, he would miss this woman! Briefly, he saw Ariane in his mind's eye. He felt himself harden further as he imagined it was her with her head in his lap, working so hard to please him. Could it be possible that the love they had for each other could evolve into something as satisfying as Melissa's relationship with Conrad?

She was sucking him now, drawing the length of him deeply into her mouth, and he allowed himself to stop thinking and concentrate on sensation. As the cab crawled through the heaving inner city streets, Jon was conscious that anyone could look in through the window of the taxi and see what was happening. He could tell from the stiff angle of the driver's head that he was aware of what was going on. Jon couldn't bring himself to care, all that mattered was that she should continue.

The ejaculate was gathering at the base of his balls now, preparing to gush into her hot, willing mouth. Melissa reached beneath him and cupped his scrotum, scratching gently at the crease with her dangerously long fingernails.

He came at once, caging a cry of triumph behind his teeth, just as they drew up outside Melissa's hotel. As the cab drew to a halt, she straightened, her eyes sparkling with mischief. Slowly, she licked her lips.

'Thank you, darling – that was lovely!' she said.

Jon barely had time to recover his breath before she kissed him quickly on the mouth, then slipped out of the cab. He watched

198

her walk away, tasting semen and her own, unique flavour on his lips.

'Where to now, guv?' the cab driver asked him, jolting him out of his stupor.

'Um . . . home, please,' Jon replied, giving the driver his address.

As soon as he stepped through the door into the flat he called home, Jon knew that Ariane wasn't there. Frowning, he wondered where she might be at that time in the evening. Had she received the fax he'd sent her telling her when he would be home?

Going over to her desk, he saw the information hanging out of her machine and wondered why she hadn't checked it. There were messages on her answerphone, too, some from the day before. It wasn't like her to ignore her phone and fax, normally she was such a tidy, methodical sort of person.

Concerned, Jon looked around him. He saw the drawings immediately. Propped up all around the room were sketches in Ariane's distinctive style, though the subject matter was not something he would ever have associated with Ariane. He picked up a line drawing of a woman kneeling, her wrists drawn behind her as if bound, her head thrown back. She was naked save for a body harness and Jon felt a stirring in his loins as he stared at the detail of the strap which fitted snugly between the lips of her sex.

'My God,' he whispered as he recognised her, 'Ariane!'

All the sketches were the same – Ariane had drawn herself, bound or lying in an attitude of abandonment, pride in her own body shrieking from every line. Then he saw the sketches she had made of Conrad, and everything fell into place.

How many times had Melissa hinted that Ariane was sleeping with Conrad? He had chosen to ignore her, unable to contemplate his fiancée discovering herself with another man as he had with Melissa. Now he could not hide from the truth and he was forced to examine his feelings.

Strangely, he felt quite calm, pleased, almost, that she had not remained the same while he had changed. The question was, were the changes they had undergone compatible with each other?

The telephone rang and he snatched it up.

'Ariane?'

'No, it's me, Melissa.'

'Melissa – is everything all right?'

'Of course. Jon, have a shower and get some sleep. Conrad wants us to meet him in two hours – I'll send a cab for you. Is that all right?'

Jon considered refusing to play Conrad's game any longer, but something told him that this was the finale, and that he wouldn't want to miss it.

'Sure. I'll see you later,' he said, then, replacing the receiver, he took Melissa's advice and headed for the bathroom.

A warm shower washed away a great deal of his weariness, but he was still tired enough to lie down on the freshly made bed – new sheets, he noticed absently – and drift quite effortlessly into sleep.

In the cab on the way to Andrew's apartment, Conrad and Andrew talked quietly while Rupert edged closer to Ariane and began to fondle her breasts. Ariane sat in rigid acquiescence, sensing that, though they did not appear to be taking any notice of her, the older men were watching her reactions. Something told her that this was some kind of test and she was determined that she should not fail it.

Rupert began to kiss her, thrusting his tongue hotly into her mouth, probing the softness of her inner cheeks.

'Open your legs for us, Angel.'

She responded at once to Conrad's low-voiced request, exposing her naked sex to their gaze. The idea of them looking at her in such a way aroused her far more than Rupert's caresses which were enthusiastic, but lacked any real skill.

'You shave her yourself?' she heard Andrew ask conversationally.

'Yes. I like to be able to see everything.'

'Mmm. Quite delicious. You see how wet she is?'

'She's always responsive.'

'To everything?'

'Of course.'

Ariane heard the smile in Conrad's voice and began to respond to Rupert's inept caresses. She felt so hot, so aroused.

'I'll look forward to finding out for myself,' she heard Andrew say. 'Here we are.'

The taxi drew to a halt and they all climbed out.

'Walk ahead of us, please, Angel,' Conrad instructed her.

Ariane walked slowly in the impossibly high heels, aware of all three men watching her. Her heart beat heavily in her chest as she imagined what each was thinking.

Andrew's apartment was situated in a complex in what used to be the dockland area. Inside, it was light and spacious, furnished quite minimally in stark black and white with the odd red accent.

Conrad and the others sat, one on each of the three black leather sofas which formed a semi-circle in the middle of the living room. In the absence of any instruction from Conrad, Ariane stood uncertainly in front of them, aware of her own tension lengthening, her apprehension growing stronger. Desire churned through her veins so that she could feel the heavy, sticky dew of her arousal lying on the surface of the skin of her inner thighs. She wondered if the men could smell the earthy, musky odour of it.

There was a large mirror on one wall, and she glanced self-consciously at her reflection. Her cheeks were very pale, apart from two hectic spots of colour high on her cheekbones. Her eyes, over-bright and overly large, reflected the intensity of her arousal and she turned away from her own image, feeling uncomfortable.

The silence seemed to go on forever as the three men lit cigarettes and Andrew poured them each a tumbler of whisky. They all appeared to have forgotten her presence, even Rupert.

Not for the first time, she asked herself what she was doing? From the start, she had realised that she could refuse to enter into any of Conrad's games at any time. No one had made her come here. But she was aware that, once she had made the decision to step inside Andrew's flat, she had agreed to leave her own will outside the door. Furthermore, though it was Andrew's apartment, Conrad was master here, she his slave. There were no choices, except his.

Perhaps that was why she had taken to his particular brand of loving so readily. Because his choices so closely mirrored her own, unspoken desires. Because she craved the shame he could so casually inflict.

The sensitive skin of her vulva moistened further and swelled as she savoured the anticipation of the punishment she sensed was to come. Anything would be better than their indifference. It didn't matter what he did, so long as it hurt. Please God, let it hurt!

'So – what are we to do with you?'

Ariane's head shot up as Conrad spoke. Carefully masking

the leap of excitement in her eyes, she stared blankly at him, a picture of passivity.

'How should we punish bad girls who are so eager to show strangers their cunts? What do you think, Rupert?'

'I think she should take off her clothes,' Rupert answered immediately.

Lord, how mundane! Ariane caught Conrad's eye and knew a fleeting moment of total accord. He was as disappointed with Rupert's lack of imagination as she.

'I think she should start by pulling her dress over her shoulders, but no more.'

Andrew's voice was bold and unequivocal. On a slight nod from Conrad, Ariane pushed the narrow strip of fabric over her shoulders. Rupert made a gesture of impatience.

'Christ, that's no good – I want to see her tits!'

The other two men ignored Rupert's crudity and Ariane stood motionless in front of them, waiting.

'Get them out,' Andrew said at last, his voice low and thick with desire. 'Pull the dress down, under your breasts.'

Ariane's hands trembled as she eased the neckline over her left breast. It was too tight to reach over the other one, and Andrew stopped her.

'Just one will do for now. What a sight!'

It was Conrad who broke the silence which descended on them.

'On your knees, Angel.'

There was a part of her, even now, which rebelled. A small portion of her which wanted to tell him to go to hell before she turned and walked out. But as she stood there, challenging him with her eyes, the last of her resistance ebbed away.

It was quite, quite delicious, the warm, melting sensation in the pit of her stomach which slowly trickled through the rest of her body. The moment of submission, the exquisite acceptance of her fate. Slowly, gracefully, she sank to her knees.

Conrad sighed, savouring the moment as she savoured it.

'All fours, Angel – that is, if you gentlemen agree?'

There was a murmur of assent, as if he had asked them to comment on the quality of the whisky. Ariane assumed the position, picturing as she did so what they could see. Her slender back was arched, like a cat, her fleshy hips tapering to her stockinged thighs. Her left breast dangled uncomfortably, so that she felt unbalanced.

'Turn around.'

She did so, presenting them with a view of her bottom. The dress had ridden up her thighs so that she knew they could see everything, from the crease between her buttocks to her moist sex below.

'Arse high. Good girl, Angel. It's a pity you didn't decide to be good earlier, then we wouldn't have to punish you, would we?'

'No,' she whispered.

'You know what I want you to do now, don't you?'

Oh yes, she knew. Once, in a rare moment of empathy, he had confided in her that this was one of his biggest thrills.

'You want me to crawl.'

'That's right. All the way to the window.'

He knew she hated this. Had to concentrate on putting one hand before the other, shuffling her knees, *left, right, left, right . . .*

The stripped pine floor was cool beneath her palms, but unkind to her stockings. She felt them rip, the ladders travelling up her thighs. The men sighed heavily, as if one.

'Ah, Angel, what a sight you are! Don't stop – crawl to the other side of the room.'

'Make her stick her arse higher in the air!' Rupert's voice was higher than normal and Ariane guessed that he had already brought his cock out of his pants.

Dipping her waist, she pushed her bottom up, feeling the cold scrape of the floorboards against her one exposed nipple. She felt clumsy, inelegant. They couldn't have devised a more effective way to humiliate her than to have her crawl about the floor, like a dog, for their entertainment.

She had reached the window now at the far side of the room. No-one spoke to her, so she crawled round in a semi-circle, careful to keep her bottom high.

'Come here,' Rupert said.

She crawled over to where Rupert was handling his penis. It was long and thick, the foreskin distended by the bulbous head. He pointed at it.

'Suck.'

Ariane buried her face in his lap, and began to lick her way along his shaft.

'I said suck,' he told her impatiently, tangling his hand in the back of her hair and holding her face still as he penetrated her mouth.

As she worked diligently on Rupert's cock, Ariane caught snippets of the conversation between Andrew and Conrad.

'She's beautiful – perfect. Where did you find her?'

'In the most unexpected of places. Swallow every drop when he comes, Angel – I shall inspect your mouth afterwards to check.'

'She seems to like it.'

'She loves it.'

His voice was heavy with emotion and Ariane's heart swelled with pride. As Rupert's sperm began to spurt to the back of her throat, she gulped at it, desperately trying not to let any escape.

'Come over to me.'

Keeping her head low, Ariane crawled over to where Conrad was waiting for her. He tipped back her head with a forefinger under her chin.

'Open,' he instructed, tapping her lips firmly with the forefinger of his other hand.

Ariane opened her mouth and suffered his inspection, As she did so, a small trickle of ejaculate escaped from the corner of her mouth. His eyes lit up.

'Oh, dear. And you were trying so hard! What shall it be, my Angel – the cane or the crop? You decide.'

Ariane thought of the pain each would inflict on her cringing flesh and opted for the more precise of the two.

'The cane, please.'

He smiled at her, pleased by the swiftness of her reply.

'Very well. First, though, I think we would enjoy watching you crawl some more, wouldn't we, Andrew?'

'Oh, yes. Knees apart, though, this time. And both breasts scraping the floor.'

He leaned across and ripped the neckline of her dress so that the other breast spilled out to join its twin. Andrew reached forward and cupped both breasts in his hands, squeezing and kneading them until Ariane moaned in mild protest.

'Bend forward again.'

She did as Andrew asked, kneeling on all fours, facing him. Sliding off the sofa, he reached for her breasts and made them swing gently. The sight of them made his breathing deepen, his fascination providing a powerful spur to Ariane's shame.

She cried out as he slapped them sharply on the underside, her cry turning into a moan of mortification as she felt her nipples harden in response.

'Oh, yes!' Andrew murmured, repeating the procedure. 'Can I use the cane on these?'

'Of course,' Conrad replied with a nonchalance which sent a frisson of alarm along Ariane's spine.

Satisfied he could return to her breasts later, Andrew sat back on his seat.

'Now you can crawl,' he told her.

Ariane began to move away from them again, her progress slower now that she was required to keep her knees apart. The men talked amongst themselves, and she felt her face flame as she listened to their comments.

'She's wet – can you see her gaping?'

'Does she like being caned?'

'No, she cries when I cane her.'

He laughed, and Ariane knew he was savouring the memory of her tears of shame.

'And you let that stop you?' This from Rupert.

Conrad laughed again.

'No. I could show you some wonderful photographs . . .'

'Another time – I want to see her marked with the cane.'

'Patience, Andrew, can't you see how much she enjoys the anticipation?'

Nevertheless, Ariane heard him stand and move to a cupboard where she presumed Andrew kept his equipment. She stopped crawling, waiting, breath held, for the sound of his approach. Her sex felt full and heavy, hanging between her legs like a ripe fruit. Longing to touch herself, she knew she dared not relieve the pressure which was building to an almost unbearable pitch. If she did so, the game would be over even before it was begun.

The first stinging blow took her breath away. Although she had promised herself she would not cry out, the second descent made her gasp. He was meticulous in his strokes, never striping the same area twice, always careful not to break the skin. There was a roaring in her ears as the pain caused by the cane built up, until she felt as though her bottom was on fire.

Andrew could not hold out to wield the cane over her breasts as he had threatened. Instead he fell on her burning behind with an incoherent groan, entering her with a savagery which took her breath away. Rupert lay on his back on the floor and began to suckle her breasts.

Ariane raised her face to Conrad as he came to kneel in front of her. He wiped away her tears with the pad of his thumb and smiled at her indulgently.

'Well done, my Angel,' he said softly. 'Would you like to come now?'

'Oh, oh yes, please,' she gasped as Andrew came and swiftly withdrew, just as Rupert rolled away from her.

Reaching down beneath her body, Conrad touched two fingers lightly against the swollen crest of her clitoris. Ariane cried out with joy as the sensations immediately began to build. Seeking her mouth with his, he kissed her deeply, circling his fingers round and round her straining bud with a steadily increasing rhythm until she was writhing on his hand.

As the first waves of orgasm crashed from her, Ariane reared up on her knees and flung her arms around his neck, clinging onto him as she rode the crest of the wave, bearing down on his fingers until the tide was past. It was so intense, so spectacular, she almost passed out.

His arms came about her and she leaned gratefully against him, drawing on his strength. Whereas moments ago Rupert and Andrew had been at the centre of her universe, essential to her in a way no two men had ever been before, now they were returned to the status of strangers. Unimportant, disregarded.

Conrad kissed her face before picking her up and carrying her over to the sofa.

'Rest a little,' he said, holding his glass to her lips so that she could drink.

Ariane gulped at the fiery liquid, watching with wide eyes as Rupert gathered Andrew in his arms. Holding the other man's face between his palms, he showered it with small kisses, finally capturing his mouth and kissing him deeply.

Andrew groaned and pressed Rupert close to him. Both men were kneeling face to face, oblivious to the discomfort of the cold pine floor and to the couple watching them from the sofa. Ariane suddenly felt awkward.

'Conrad, I—'

'Ssh,' he interrupted her, pressing a finger against her lips to silence her. 'Having an audience is part of the pleasure to them.'

'But—'

'Watch.'

Reluctantly, Ariane turned her attention back to the two men, who were now undressing each other with a grace which could only have been carefully choreographed. Ariane had never really even thought about what two men might do together, and she wasn't at all sure that she wanted to watch. Conrad, though, held her fast, his fingertips describing sensuous little circles on the upper part of her arm, making her shiver.

Glancing surreptitiously at him from beneath her lashes, she saw that he was absorbed in watching the two men kiss and caress each other. Could it be that he was perhaps a little *too* interested, that maybe he really didn't find the prospect of making love to her very exciting?

Remembering how he had been perfectly capable of fucking

Charlotte, Ariane dismissed the thought almost as soon as it was formed. Focusing once more on Andrew and Rupert, she pressed herself closer to him, as if to absorb some of the arousal she could sense churning through his veins, hoping she might divert some of it in her direction.

From the smaller living room where Melissa had led him when they had arrived, Jon watched Ariane's face through the two-way mirror. He had thought she'd seen him at the beginning, when she had stared so hard at her reflection, but quickly realised that she was unaware of the mirror's function.

From her reaction to Conrad, he could see that the other man had trained her to respond in the way he desired, and that she enjoyed pleasing him. Watching the cane striping her buttocks had made him feel awed and it was all he could do not to make himself known so that he could take over.

Now she was curled in Conrad's arms, watching the two men who were kissing passionately on the floor. As they all watched, Andrew assumed the position Ariane had taken only moments before while Rupert pulled his trousers to his knees and thrust into him.

'God, they're enthusiastic, aren't they, darling?'

Melissa's voice held amusement. Jon had been aware of her watching him watching Ariane, and he turned to her now.

'Did you know about this?' he asked her.

'Does it matter?'

Jon gazed at her, marvelling as always at her beauty, weighing her words carefully.

'No,' he concluded at last, 'I don't suppose it does.'

Melissa smiled, her soft hands fluttering over his erection.

'Don't you want to go and claim Ariane?' she asked him.

Jon glanced back into the living room and saw that Ariane and Conrad were now kissing deeply. As he watched, Conrad picked her up and carried her out of the room. Frowning, he turned back to Melissa.

'Where's he taking her?'

'To a bedroom I should imagine. Shall we follow?'

Jon hesitated as it occurred to him that Ariane might not be pleased to see him before she had been introduced to the idea that he, too, had changed.

'You ought to know, darling, that so far Conrad has refrained from actually cuckolding you.'

Jon smiled at her mocking use of the old-fashioned term. Could it really be possible?

'Apparently, Ariane is more than ready to take that extra step. I suggest if you want her to be yours, you act now.'

Jon nodded.

'Let's go.'

In the dimly lit bedroom, Ariane was ecstatic that, at last, Conrad was caressing her as she had always wanted him to. Surely this must be but a prelude to their coming together at last? He wouldn't deny her now – would he?

'I'm so proud of you, Angel,' he murmured, moving his lips against the soft fall of her hair. 'You were magnificent in there.'

Ariane absorbed his praise, glowing with pride that she had not disappointed him.

'Thank you,' she whispered against his mouth.

'For what?' Pulling back slightly, he smiled indulgently at her.

'For helping me to discover my true sexual potential. If I hadn't met you, I would never have known the true meaning of bliss.'

She sighed deeply as Conrad's hands roamed her body. Holding up her arms, she helped him to pull off what was left of her dress, gasping as he rolled down her stockings and his warm breath tickled her mound of Venus.

Conrad raised his head and looked at her and suddenly the laughter caught in her throat. A bolt of desire shot through her, savage and uncontrollable and she felt her sex pulse into life again.

'Please . . . ?' she whispered.

'Please, Angel? What is it you want?' he asked her, echoing his words to her that first time he had come to her flat.

This time, Ariane was neither shy, nor shameful. Looking him straight in the eye, Ariane told him exactly what she wanted.

'I want you inside me, Conrad. I want you to fuck me.'

His eyes darkened and he turned her bodily so that her bottom was presented to him.

'Up on your knees,' he whispered thickly. 'Legs apart. That's it, Angel – open yourself for me. You want me to fuck you?'

'Yes,' she murmured feverishly, 'oh, yes!'

'Like this – from behind?'

The suspense was killing her, making her ache for release.

'Any way you want to!' she cried.

'All right. Lay your cheek against the pillow and close your eyes.'

Ariane obeyed his instructions automatically, seduced by the tenor of his voice.

'Stay very still, my Angel, while your master fucks you.'

She felt the tip of his cock probe the opening to her womb, his hands holding her still. His fingers dug into the fleshy covering on her hips as, with one, sure thrust, he entered her.

Ariane cried out, hardly daring to believe that he was giving her what she wanted at last. Pushing back against him, she deepened the penetration, almost fainting with pleasure as he reached round to rub at her clitoris.

His touch was firm and assured, but not quite as she had expected it to be. There was something familiar about the cock moving inside, something she recognised about the smell of his skin.

The sound of another woman's low-voiced sigh made her open her eyes. She sucked in her breath as she saw a naked woman sitting astride a man on a rattan chair.

'Conrad!' she whispered.

His head was thrown back and his handsome face was contorted into a rictus of ecstasy as the woman moved up and down. Ariane could see his cock, wet and shiny with her juices, pumping in and out of the woman's body.

And she knew at once why everything felt so familiar.

'Jon!' she cried, trying to squirm in his embrace.

'Be still!' he said.

There was a note of command which she had never heard in his voice before, a self-assurance that he had never shown in the past. There was a difference, too, in the way he thrust into her willing body. There was none of the reverence she had come to expect in his movements, rather he was taking her, quite mercilessly, without a thought, it seemed, for her comfort.

'Jon—'

'Bear down – I want you to come as I do.'

'Oh!' she sighed as she instinctively obeyed him.

A kaleidoscope of colours seemed to explode behind her closed eyelids as her orgasm broke. At the same time she was conscious of Jon's cock spasming inside her, his hot emission branding her as his.

His lips pressed against the nobbly protrusions of her spine, kissing a path up to the nape of her neck.

'Ariane,' he whispered, his voice quite different now, 'my love . . .'

As he slipped out of her, she turned in his arms and he smothered her face with kisses.

'You saw, didn't you? In the living room?' she asked when she had had time to catch her breath.

Jon's face darkened and an expression crept into his eyes which she recognised. A familiar churning began in the pit of her stomach.

'Yes, I saw. Now I know what you have been doing while I've been away, I shall have to devise some suitable . . . punishments for you.'

Ariane stared at him. Could it really be that Jon had always been the other half to her other that Conrad had described?

'Oh, yes,' she breathed.

The sound of encroaching ecstasy from the corner of the room attracted their attention and they turned as one to look at Conrad and Melissa. Completely oblivious to Jon and Ariane, they appeared to be riding the wave together, their faces held close, their long, dark hair obscuring their expressions.

'Have you and Melissa . . .'

'I understand now,' Jon interrupted her.

Ariane wanted to protest that he hadn't answered her question, that she needed to know if he had been involved with the beautiful brunette who was giving Conrad so much pleasure. Then she realised in a rare flash of perfect clarity that she needed to know nothing, it was enough that he had come home to her, that he was willing to be her very own, loving master.

As they watched, Conrad and Melissa moved apart. Conrad

removed the gold ring he wore on the small finger of his left hand and handed it to Melissa. Jon smiled, recognising it as the twin to the ring that Melissa wore through her labia.

'That reminds me,' he said, reaching over the bed for his discarded jacket, 'I have a gift for you.'

He drew out a gold paper bag and handed it to Ariane. He watched her face as she tipped it up and the small gold ring with the sapphire teardrop fell into her palm.

'It's beautiful,' she said, holding it up so that the dull light of the bedside lamp reflected off it. 'But I don't understand . . . what is it?'

Jon smiled at her.

'I want you to wear it as my mark. Melissa – will you show Ariane your rings?'

'With pleasure!'

Melissa moved over to the bed and spread her legs wide. Ariane gasped as she saw the gold ring piercing her labia. Conrad moved forward and, taking the second ring, inserted it carefully in its rightful place.

'You see?' Jon said. 'Will you be pierced so that you can wear this for me?'

Ariane hesitated for only a moment, then she nodded.

'Yes,' she said, 'I'll wear it.'

The idea of wearing Jon's ring in such a way aroused her all over again.

'Can we go home now?'

Jon glanced at Melissa and Conrad.

'We'll meet up again before you leave,' he said.

Conrad nodded and held out his hand. Jon grasped it and the two men shook hands, silently acknowledging their mutual debt. Melissa smiled at Ariane and, impulsively, Ariane embraced her, feeling quite emotional. Finally, Conrad turned to her.

'Take care – Ariane,' he said.

It was the first time he had ever used her name. Ariane felt a pang of sorrow that she would not be his Angel any more. Then Jon helped her dress and wrapped his jacket around her, and she knew that the sorrow would quickly pass. Looking up at him, she smiled.

'Take me home,' she said softly.

Jon nodded.

'Always,' he replied.

Allowing herself to lean into the security of his embrace, Ariane left the room without so much as a backward glance.

## *Adult Fiction for Lovers from Headline LIAISON*

| | | |
|---|---|---|
| SLEEPLESS NIGHTS | Tom Crewe & Amber Wells | £4.99 |
| THE JOURNAL | James Allen | £4.99 |
| THE PARADISE GARDEN | Aurelia Clifford | £4.99 |
| APHRODISIA | Rebecca Ambrose | £4.99 |
| DANGEROUS DESIRES | J. J. Duke | £4.99 |
| PRIVATE LESSONS | Cheryl Mildenhall | £4.99 |
| LOVE LETTERS | James Allen | £4.99 |

*All Headline Liaison books are available at your local bookshop or newsagent, or can be ordered direct from the publisher. Just tick the titles you want and fill in the form below. Prices and availability subject to change without notice.*

Headline Book Publishing, Cash Sales Department, Bookpoint, 39 Milton Park, Abingdon, OXON, OX14 4TD, UK. If you have a credit card you may order by telephone – 01235 400400.

Please enclose a cheque or postal order made payable to Bookpoint Ltd to the value of the cover price and allow the following for postage and packing: UK & BFPO: £1.00 for the first book, 50p for the second book and 30p for each additional book ordered up to a maximum charge of £3.00. OVERSEAS & EIRE: £2.00 for the first book, £1.00 for the second book and 50p for each additional book.

Name ........................................................................................

Address ...................................................................................

..................................................................................................

..................................................................................................

If you would prefer to pay by credit card, please complete:
Please debit my Visa/Access/Diner's Card/American Express
(Delete as applicable) card no:

| | | | | | | | | | | | | | | | |
|---|---|---|---|---|---|---|---|---|---|---|---|---|---|---|---|
| | | | | | | | | | | | | | | | |

Signature .................................................... Expiry Date ..............